She felt his anger change to passion

"Daniel," Carly breathed against his lips.

"What?" He raised his face heavy with desire and gazed down into her eyes. "Tell him, Charlotte. Tell Bram Calthrop to get out of your life."

"I—" She stopped and felt his body stiffen, then he moved away. "I can't," she whispered.

"Which tells me everything I need to know," Daniel remarked with a vicious pleasantness. "Obviously you want him more than me. Or is it his money you love?" She couldn't answer, and he sneered, "Good night, then, Charlotte. I know we share a house, but try to keep out of my sight!"

He went and, this time, she let him go. What was the point? Would Daniel—would anyone in his mood—believe Bram was blackmailing her?

These books may be available at your local bookseller.

Don't miss any of our special offers. Write to us at the following address for information on our newest releases.

Harlequin Reader Service
P.O. Box 52040, Phoenix, AZ 85072-2040
Canadian address: P.O. Box 2800, Postal Station A,
5170 Yonge St., Willowdale, Ont. M2N 6J3

Emperor Stone

Sheila Strutt

Harlequin Books

TORONTO • NEW YORK • LONDON
AMSTERDAM • PARIS • SYDNEY • HAMBURG
STOCKHOLM • ATHENS • TOKYO • MILAN

Original hardcover edition published in 1984
by Mills & Boon Limited

ISBN 0-373-02699-4

Harlequin Romance first edition June 1985

CHAPTER ONE

IT took ten seconds to destroy what it had taken her ten years of her life to achieve.

'Are you coming for a drink?' His reflection framed in the naked electric light bulbs on all four sides of the dressing room mirror, Bram studied her.

'I guess so!' Carly Mason went on wiping make-up from her face.

'You don't sound too enthused!'

'I'm not!' She rubbed along her nose.

'What about the others? They'll be expecting us?'

'So?' Carly pulled another tissue from the box.

Bram crossed one long leg over the other and gave one of his quiet smiles. 'They'll think you're being English and stand-offish if we don't turn up!'

Carly shrugged, the thin straps of her slip sliding on bare shoulders. Bram must have sat in her dressing room like this dozens of times, but it still made her uncomfortable to be part-dressed in front of him. 'Backer's perks!' he had said the one time she had mentioned it.

'Some of them will, I suppose!' she said now. 'But it'll be you they'll miss, not me!'

'And that doesn't bother you?' He seemed amused.

'Not especially!' It did, but the last thing she intended was to let it show.

Instead, she concentrated on removing the last traces of heavy theatrical make-up from her hair line. One day, she was determined, there would be a dressing room with a star pinned to the door—and a shower. That was the worst part of acting. Going home with make-up still on your skin. She always felt greasy and unclean until she got underneath that stream of water.

Against the background of Bram's knowing smile, she screwed the cap back on the bottle of baby oil she had been using to remove her make-up, dumped the last of the used tissues into the wicker basket beside her feet and put the bottle of baby oil into her canvas tote.

'Two camps, eh?' Bram leaned back in the one armchair the small dressing room provided and inspected the length of sock between his brightly polished shoe and the knife edged crease of his trouser leg. All she could see was the top of a smooth brown head and the foreshortened tip of a patrician Boston Brahmin nose. Brampton Calthrop III. An unlikely angel, particularly in this fringe theatre world. 'Americans versus Brits!' Bram elaborated.

'Maybe!' Carly tried even harder to be non-committal. It was her relationship to Bram that had created the ever present feeling of resentment among the other members of the cast, not her nationality or her accent. That was inflexion perfect; growing up with an American mother had seen to that. In fact, Bram's normal speaking voice sounded more English than hers did when she was on stage.

That had been the initial root of his attraction; drawing her to him at that party in New York, an island of identity in an otherwise all American crowd. It had made it easy to relate and even easier to accept an invitation to dinner afterwards. Finding out that, far from English, Bram was an east coast Bostonian born and bred had hardly mattered then. She had been Dan-sick—homesick—Carly firmly substituted the word. She had not been Dan-sick since she had walked out of a particular flat in England—the real England—almost ten years earlier. Daniel had just been in her mind that night because she had just had news that the divorce was finally going to go through.

'Will you be long?'

'No! Not very!' For a moment, it was an effort to remember exactly who it was reaching for the half empty bottle of champagne in the cooler beside his chair. 'I'll be ready in five minutes!' It was Bram. Who else could it be?

Carly began picking up the jars and bottles she had set out with such ritualistic precision three months earlier. Every actor had his, or her, own personal superstition—at least, all the actors she had ever met—and hers was to spread a cloth on her dressing table on the last night of rehearsal and set out her make-up in a very particular order. It then stayed there, in exactly that same pattern, until the run was over.

Everything she now picked up left its shape in

the thin layer of face powder that had drifted
down and settled on the cloth. She finished
packing the last of her stage make-up into her
tote bag, picked up the cloth—no longer white
but streaked with brown and orange—shook it,
folded it and put it with the rest into her bag.
Another production over. Another part learned
and performed and the knowledge and experience
she had gained stored away in her brain's
computer against the day when, far from relying
on Bram's patronage, producers would be
scrambling to book her in her own right.

Had it really been twelve weeks since the play
had opened; eight years since she had first met
Bram and ten—almost—since she had slammed a
particular door for the last time?

Carly firmly zipped her tote bag shut.
Nostalgia was dangerous. The last night of a run
which she had not particularly enjoyed was
hardly cause for going so far back in time,
especially when her future was all planned out.

'I'm ready!'

'Good! Except——' Bram's pale blue eyes ran
over her with their own private smile, 'I hardly
think that what you're wearing is exactly
suitable. At least, not for a party!' he added
pointedly.

Carly stood up, feeling the weight of thick,
dark hair against her bare shoulders. 'Yes, well, I
still have to put on my street clothes!'

This was ridiculous! She wasn't naked, or even
near it in the heavy black nylon slip. One good
thing about the current vogue of nostalgia for the

fifties was that at least the plays demanded substantial clothes. If it had been *Hair* they had been reviving, or any one of the productions of the liberated sixties, she would probably be wearing little more than body make-up.

But it was still difficult to walk past Bram to get to the curtained off partition in the corner and she was more than conscious of him there behind the curtain as she took off the black slip and put it in the basket for the dresser and then put on her own slip, dress and shoes.

Not that Bram had ever pressed home his advantage or explicitly demanded payment for his sponsorship of her career but it was there, all the same, in the air between them. She might be, as Bram often said, ambitious, but that didn't close her eyes to the fact that there were as many actresses as talented and attractive and many more with the advantage of having been born in the United States.

'I think the rest of the company are probably going to Ginny's!' A theatre bar, one of the kind in San Francisco that sprang up every year only to close down and reappear under a different name the following season. Quickly fastening buttons, Carly went back to the safe topic of the last night party. 'But then,' she realised, 'you probably know! I expect you're picking up the tab!'

'Maybe!' She didn't have to see him, she could feel the exact spot where his eyes were resting on the curtain. One day soon, another bill would be due for payment. 'But that doesn't mean we have to go there!' he said casually.

'Where shall we go, then?'

'Wherever you like, my dear!'

Where was her purse? Carly hunted for the leather clutch underneath the rack of costumes the dresser was probably waiting to take down and check for the last time.

Bram spoke into the pause. 'How about The Wharf?'

The Wharf! Full of people and quite safe! Carly hadn't realised just how tense she was until she felt herself relax.

It wasn't that she was scared of Bram. Grateful, yes, and sometimes disbelieving of her good luck, but never scared of him.

Her purse appeared on the narrow ledge beneath the rack of costumes she would never wear again and Carly picked it up and checked her reflection in the mirror in the flap.

Dark hair, brown eyes, a strong full mouth of naturally dark red, all added up to form a face striking enough to be seen at its best behind the footlights. Charlotte Mason—now known as Carly—actress and looking any year up to five less than her actual thirty. No! Not quite thirty. She still had a few months to go before she reached that particular watershed. Married, divorced and now just on the brink of taking off with her career and all because of Bram.

She knew he wanted her, was even now prepared to marry her. At first, it had just been wanting; that night at the party and then, a year or more later when he had tracked her down and unexpectedly got in touch with her again, they had played a game. At least, on his side, it had been a game. On hers, it had been something much more fundamental. A distaste, a reluctance to turn herself into the sort of person she would not like to have to face in her mirror in the morning, that had refused to allow her to give in and sleep her way to a career. And it had perhaps been this that had made Bram reassess his first impressions and see her not just as an aspiring actress but as a future wife.

Mrs Brampton Calthrop III. A lot of girls at that first party would doubtless have been only too pleased to settle for that particular billing rather than see their own name in the brightest lights.

It had been a theatre party, full of actors, actresses and theatre people generally. To this day, she was not quite sure what Bram had been doing there but the result was that here she was, in San Francisco, finishing in a play that Bram had backed and paid for. A play that had got 'newcomer' Carly Mason rave notices in all the papers and paved the way not just for a Broadway opening but a chance at Hollywood, the biggest prize of all.

'I'm ready!' It had been a mistake to pull the curtain back and stand there. The pale blue dress was electric against her darker skin and eyes and it must have looked as if she was trying to make an entrance. She turned away from the look of raw urgency on Bram's face and let the curtain drop. 'I'm ready!' she said awkwardly.

Bram was almost fifty and Bram was a

gentleman but Bram was also very much a man. In all the miles and all the time that had brought them across America from New York to San Francisco his image of her might well have changed from actress and potential mistress to actress and potential wife, but the wanting was still there. Scratch the surface and the sexuality beneath the thousand dollar suit appeared.

Brampton Calthrop III, old money Boston millionaire, able to travel, fall in love, do anything he liked and still she could not give herself to him. Every time she thought in terms of marriage, she saw a door. The door she had slammed almost ten years earlier.

'Then if you're ready, we'd better go!' Bram rose abruptly from his chair. 'Have you got a wrap?'

'No! Will I need one?' This time, what she said was wrong.

Bram immediately pulled her to him. 'No,' he said. 'I shouldn't think so!'

She felt every inch of him against her as he guided her through the door.

''Night, Miss Mason—Mr Calthrop!' The drama student who kept stage door until his chance as an actor also came along, grinned at them from his cubby hole as they went past.

Bram stopped. 'Aren't you going to the party?' he said shortly. 'I thought you'd be off by now!'

'Yes, sure!' For a second, the boy looked awkward and the thought crossed Carly's mind that he might have stayed on the offchance of a word alone with Bram. Bram, after all, had influence; Bram had power and it was a cut-throat world in which the boy was trying to make his way. All the cast knew of Bram's patronage of her; there was absolutely no reason why it should not also be common knowledge among the backstage staff and crew. 'I guess I thought I'd wait until everyone had gone before I went across!' The boy looked at Bram with hopeful eyes. 'I'll see you later than, Mr Calthrop? At Ginny's? Oh! and thanks for inviting me!'

Bram took firm hold of Carly's elbow. 'You're welcome! So!' He put the question with a smile as they went through the stage door. 'No looking back? It's okay, Frank!' He waved the emerging chauffeur back behind the wheel of the Mercedes limousine parked across the sidewalk. 'I think I'm capable of opening a door!'

His arm brushed across Carly's breast as he leaned forward and she got quickly into the back seat.

'No!' she said. 'No looking back! I don't believe in it!'

The play was done, finished, over, like so much else in her life and she had learned the lesson about not looking back almost ten years before. What was done could not be altered; what was shattered could not be repaired and, besides, she had much more to look forward to than to regret.

This play, in the fringe theatre of San Francisco, had been just a stepping stone. Bram was arranging an off-Broadway production for their next venture and after that, it would very probably be Hollywood. Who was it who had once said that the only way to be a star was in Hollywood? She didn't know and she didn't care—any more than she really cared what the people with whom she had just finished working really thought of her. All she knew was that, in a few months' time, Hollywood would not just be beckoning, it would be there, in the form of a pen and a contract for her to sign on the dotted line.

'The Wharf, Frank!' Bram settled back in his corner of the leather seat and gave the instruction to the chauffeur. 'Pier 21, I think!' His eyes slid round to Carly, indulgent and amused. 'Will that do!'

'Yes,' she said, 'and thank you, Bram! About Ginny's, I mean,' she explained quickly, 'and about the party. You would probably have liked to go!'

'Not if you don't! Anything you want, Carly, you know that!'

Her debt was building. She could see the urgency and hear the invitation in his voice. Why couldn't she respond? A quick kiss on the cheek would be enough. It would be small enough payment, after all, for everything Bram had done for her. Instead, she turned her head and watched the late night street go by.

Cable cars, lights, people, San Francisco! She had never in a million years dreamed she would be there. She had almost had to pinch herself when they had flown in against the sun and she had had her first sight of a city like a pile of pearls, piled on an oyster shell and floating on a shot silk sea.

And yet, in many ways, it was strange that she should even find it strange that she should be here, on this strip of the Pacific coast, thousands of miles from almost everyone she knew.

England, where she had been born, Germany, Cyprus, the Far East; anywhere there had been a call for the services of the Canadian contingent of the United Nations Peace Keeping Corps had, at some time or another, been her home when she was growing up.

A Canadian father with the Canadian armed forces and a mother of mixed Spanish-American ancestry had been the sole unchanging nucleus of her ever-changing world. At least her mother would be quite at home here in San Francisco's Spanish atmosphere of red tiled roofs and cream washed buildings. Anna Paz Sabillon—Mrs Curtis Mason—from whom Carly had inherited her smooth brown complexion and thick, dark hair.

Watching the streets go by, her thoughts began to wander. Her mother, a house they had once had in Cyprus, the flat in London. She sat up straight. That part of her life was over. She was in America, taking advantage of the citizenship she got automatically from her mother. A whole new person with a whole new career ahead of her.

'You could always go on to Ginny's without me later!' Conscience kept her harking back to the subject of the party.

Bram smiled easily. 'By that time, everyone

will be too far gone to notice whether I'm there or not! Relax!' His hand came out to cover hers. 'Don't worry! You don't want to go? That's fine! You've no need to justify yourself!' He paused. 'Not to me, at least!'

Carly wished she could take her hand away. The boy who kept stage door would notice, and so would everybody else, if Bram did not turn up at Ginny's. They would also notice she wasn't there—and draw their own conclusions.

It was hot, suddenly, in spite of the air conditioning in the car.

Well, let them draw their own conclusions, she thought defiantly. She was talented and attractive and, at the age of thirty in a highly competitive and cut-throat business, she was at last going to succeed. After ten years, it was all going to come true.

'Bram!' She looked up and looked away, unable to face the urgency in his face. 'You know I'm grateful, don't you?' she finished awkwardly.

'Of course!' His voice was husky. 'Of course I do!'

The Mercedes was going more slowly now as they neared The Wharf and people spilled out from the sidewalks across the street. Once it had been just that. A fisherman's wharf for the crab and shrimp boats bringing in their catches from the Ocean and the Bay. The boats still came in but the whole area had been given a face lift. There were restaurants now and stores for tourists and sidewalk salesmen and, as the limousine went past, Carly saw heads turn and faces peer at the black tinted windows.

A car like that must mean someone famous or important. Carly drew further back into her corner. No one could see in—modern technology had taken care of that—and it was ridiculous but—she felt guilty.

'What's wrong?' Her tension transmitted itself through Bram's fingers.

'Nothing,' she lied. 'I'm just tired, that's all!'

Bram grinned. 'What you need is champagne!'

The car nosed its way through the last remaining crowds and pulled up outside a restaurant less brightly lit than most; a dowager in all the showgirl glitter of The Wharf.

The chauffeur got out and opened the door.

'About an hour, I should think, Frank!' Bram's hand was once more possessively beneath her elbow. 'Miss Mason needs an early night!'

To her tight-stretched nerves, the concern had double meaning; a hope that was always there. Trying not to make it obvious, she slipped her arm away, only to have Bram take her hand.

'Okay, Mr Calthrop, I'll come back then!' The main door to the restaurant was already opening by the time the chauffeur spoke.

Prices kept Pier 21 less crowded than the other wharfside restaurants. Dinner for two could—and often did—cost a hundred dollars. Prices and an unwritten policy that barred entry to any and everyone who could not satisfy the maitre d's acute antennae as to their wealth and social standing. For such would-be diners, empty tables visible from the doorway were, always and 'regrettably' reserved.

On both counts, though, Bram passed with flying colours.

'Good evening, Mr Calthrop!' The black coated maitre d's antennae were positively ecstatic. 'Miss Mason,' he bowed, 'a pleasure to see you here again!' He went on bowing them to a mirrored table in an alcove.

'We'll skip cocktails, Max!' Bram beckoned to the *sommelier* with his badge of office of silver chain and miniature silver ladle glinting against the dazzling starched white of his shirt front.

'Good evening, *monsieur—madame*!' A wine list was proffered but Bram waved it away.

'Just bring champagne,' he ordered. 'Chilled and good but otherwise your choice!'

'Of course, *monsieur*!' The man bowed and withdrew.

The tables on either side of them were empty. Another facet of the restaurant's policy. Just as theatres, no matter how popular or overbooked the show, always kept a few house seats available for last minute, important bookings, Pier 21 was also always ready to welcome a President—or a Queen. Carly had quickly learned how royalist the average republican American could be.

'To the future!' The champagne brought and poured and the bottle, with its napkin round its neck standing in an ice filled silver cooler at his side, Bram raised his narrow tulip shaped glass and toasted her.

'To the future!' Carly obediently copied him.

'What's wrong?' Bram was quick to notice.

'Nothing!' She tried a smile. 'Nothing! I'm just tired!'

And depressed; even though she shouldn't be depressed. True, the run of this particular play was over but New York lay ahead and this time, not as the leading actress in a revival but as the star of a tailor-made production Bram had specially commissioned.

'I'm sorry, Bram!' In the mirrored alcove, a dark haired woman in a designer dress—a woman who had everything—spread her fingers on the white starched table cloth in a gesture of despair. 'I was thinking about the play!' She tried to explain her sudden *malaise* away. 'I *am* grateful! I really am!'

'There's no need!' Bram dismissed the huge amount of money necessary to mount and stage even a small Broadway production with an easy smile. 'You've no need to be grateful, you would have made it on your own!'

'Perhaps!' Carly fiddled with her glass. That was something she now would never know.

It was capricious to the point of folly—flying in the face of fortune—to wish, perhaps, that Bram had not entered her life exactly when he had.

She had been making it; not in a big way, maybe, but she had at last been making some sort of mark. Two years after . . . Daniel! Suddenly his face was there, vivid in her mind's eye! . . . Two years after . . . Carly wrenched her mind back to its original track; she had uprooted herself from England and come to America, she had at last been making some sort of mark on the world on which she had set her sights.

It might have been just commercials and small parts in television plays but she had been getting there and she had been doing it on her own until Bram had come along and made any further effort superfluous.

A waiter materialised at their table and Bram glanced at her above his copy of the double folio menu.

'What are you going to have?'

'I don't know!' Carly looked down. Her copy of the menu had no prices. In Pier 21, women were not permitted to concern themselves with cost. 'Maybe a Crab Louis!'

'With a little vichyssoise with watercress to start? Or a pâté?' the waiter prompted. 'The house pâté is very good!'

'No!' She heard her sharp voice. 'Just a Crab Louis!' And then, to take the edge out of her reply, 'I'm not too hungry!' Crab Louis might be considered just a snack, but it was still a whole shelled crab in a beautifully presented lettuce with tomato, cucumber, scallion and a house dressing.

'Crab Louis, then, and lobster, plainly broiled with butter!' Bram settled it and dismissed the man. 'I thought perhaps you were disappointed we had to go back to New York?' He picked up the thread of their earlier conversation.

'No, of course not!' Again, another smile. 'Why should I be?'

'Because I promised you Hollywood!' Bram's eyes glowed above his glass.

'Yes, I know!' Had she really been depressed?

It seemed impossible as she faced Bram with her own dreams shining in her eyes. 'I'm grateful! Really grateful but——' something in his taut expression made her turn her head, '—I seem to be making a habit of saying that!'

'And I seem to be making a habit of saying you have no need!' In the pause between one word and the next, his whole voice changed. 'Carly,' he said thickly, 'you know that anything you want . . .?'

'Some bread, *madame*?'

It took a second for it to register. One moment, there had just been Bram, leaning across the table with urgency etched in every line of his long, patrician face and the next, a waiter had appeared, serving Crab Louis and offering a covered basket of warm rolls.

'No! No, thank you!'

If looks could kill, the waiter would be dead. Carly saw it, even if the man did not, that venomous expression on Bram's face.

Bram liked to play the part of the playboy businessman but, in fact, he was a power in several other fields. It had vanished immediately he had realised she was there but she had seen that expression once or twice before when she had walked into his New York office and surprised him on the telephone. Outwardly, he could not be more urbane and charming but, underneath that smooth façade, Brampton Calthrop III was not a man to be lightly crossed.

'More wine, *madame*?'

The covered basket of rolls had vanished and

the waiter was now offering the bottle of champagne.

She had barely touched her glass but, 'Yes! Yes, please!' Anything to take the sudden chill out of her bones.

Through the window and behind the waiter's arm, she could see the lights of the Golden Gate Bridge stretching across the Bay in a sparkling filigree but Alcatraz was also out there in the darkness behind those lights, the prison island on which men had paid the price for the decisions and behaviour that had brought them there, just as she one day would have to pay the price for the success which Bram had bought, and paid for.

Carly picked up her glass and shook her head impatiently. What was she thinking of? The price Bram was demanding was hardly incarceration in one of America's toughest prisons—it was a future as an actress and his wife.

'I thought,' behind her glass, she could see Bram's fingers resting on the tablecloth, 'I thought we might drive back to New York!'

'Drive back?' Her mouth was dry.

'Why not?' Bram was absolutely casual. 'It'll take a few days but it'll be a nice break for you before rehearsals start.'

'Yes, I suppose so!' Carly took the plunge. She owed him something, after all. Were a few days—and nights—really too big a price to pay? 'It's odd, isn't it?' She went rattling on around the point. 'I've never driven through the States! In all the years I've lived here, I've never really been too far from New York—until now, of course!'

She had to look up and face him and her laugh was much too bright. 'Perhaps we could stop off in New Orleans—or the Grand Canyon!' She saw his look of satisfaction and quickly lowered her eyes. 'I've always wanted to see that!' she finished lamely.

'Hey! Hang on!' Bram was all indulgence. 'Have you any idea how far those two places are apart?'

'No!' She still only had to say it. Not no to distances but no to the whole idea of the trip. Nothing had exactly been spelled out in words— that had never been Bram's way—he would be willing to pretend that it had all been a game.

They could still fly back to New York. Things between them could still go on exactly as they were except that the little silences would be more difficult to end and the feeling that she was somehow cheating him more difficult to ignore. As for the rest, it was as ridiculous to think that Bram would withdraw his support of her career as it was ridiculous to wish that she could go back ten years and somehow start again.

Damn Daniel! Damn Daniel Stone!

'To Colorado and the Grand Canyon!' She deliberately raised her glass and toasted him.

'To Colorado!' Bram said thickly.

'*Mesdames! Messieurs!*' The maitre d' with all his French Creole was seating a party at one of the adjoining tables. Not quite the President and his wife but two men and two women filling the alcove with well-bred social chat.

Bram's eyebrows drew together and a look of

sheer annoyance crossed his face. 'Have you finished?' he said curtly.

Carly looked down at the Crab Louis almost untouched on her plate. 'Yes!' she said.

'Then let's get out of here!'

Paying a bill took no time when all it needed was a signature. Soon—too soon—they were standing on the sidewalk outside the restaurant.

'Frank shouldn't be too far away!' Bram scanned the passing crowds, looking for the limousine. He brightened. 'That looks like him! On the far side! You wait here!' He gave her arm a possessive squeeze. 'I'll go get him!'

One minute he was there, Brampton Calthrop III, future lover, future husband, future life, threading his way through the traffic and the crowds and then she lost him.

A young couple wandered past. A couple who would most certainly not have gained admission to Pier 21. He was in jeans and she had a long skirt but they were looking at each other—Carly turned her head away from that very private look—just as she must have looked at Daniel all those years ago, waiting—hoping—that he was going to ask her to marry him.

With Daniel, there had never been any feeling that she was in control. He took or left, exactly as he chose. Even then she had been ambitious for her career but, from the moment she saw Daniel, nothing mattered. For a time, she had wanted nothing if the choice was to be his wife.

Damn Daniel! Damn! Damn! Damn! The couple went on past and she barely heard the screech of brakes. She saw the crowds, however, and she saw them running to one spot.

Bram! She knew even before she got there and pushed her way through to the front so that she could see the figure lying half underneath the refrigerated truck. 'North Western California Fish Processing.' She was no more aware of the sign painted on its side than she was aware until much, much later that what she had been struggling for ten years to achieve had taken ten seconds to destroy.

Perhaps the two thoughts came together when the police later questioned her. For the moment, all she knew as she ran and pushed her way through the crowds surrounding him was that Bram, half hidden underneath the truck, was dead.

CHAPTER TWO

'You realise, of course, Miss Mason, that any *personal* commitments Mr Brampton Calthrop may have undertaken have now been reassessed by the family?'

'Yes! Of course!' For those first few days, the fact that Bram had been alive had been enough. Hovering between life and death in intensive care; willing him as she stood and watched, hour after hour, through the plate glass window to keep the heartbeat showing steadily on the monitor beside his bed.

Reaction had come later; feelings of relief and guilt because of that relief. There would be no trip through the heartland of America, no payment for all Bram had done for her. Whatever she felt for him, it was not enough to be his wife. It was almost a relief to hear the Calthrop family lawyer saying that the family had withdrawn from one of their member's crazy impulse to back a Broadway play.

'Come in!' She did not turn from the white and gold princess telephone when the knock came on the door. 'Yes,' she said, 'of course I understand.'

There was to be no play. Her suite at the hotel was safe for a few more days—Bram's largesse again. He had been over-generous with his booking on her behalf and she was secure until the week's end.

After that, however, she had no idea of her future plans. All she knew was they no longer included a Broadway opening.

Footsteps came up behind her on the thick pile carpet and then stopped. Still she didn't turn. 'Leave the bill. I'll sign it later!' Lunch or dinner—she had lost track of time—but room service must have delivered one or the other.

'Will you ask them—the family, I mean, to let me know how Mr Calthrop is progressing?' Huddled over the telephone, Carly sought the lawyer's help.

The moment he had been fit to move, a private jet had flown into San Francisco and taken Bram away. The family once more! Bram had never talked too much about them but they had been there, waiting to reclaim the member who had strayed.

The Calthrops were in banking and in politics—not up front in the limelight of the hustings but quietly and powerfully behind the scenes. Privacy was a religion. Carly could just imagine their reaction to the news that the senior member of the family was travelling round the country backing plays, just as she could imagine exactly what they thought of her; the scheming, gold-digging actress out of nowhere who had bewitched Bram to the point of lunacy.

No Calthrop had ever been involved in the theatre; no Calthrop would ever consider marrying a woman who was on the stage.

'I'll ask them, of course, to advise you of Mr Calthrop's progress but I can't guarantee that the family will be willing . . .!' Over the telephone, the lawyer's voice trailed away.

'No! Of course not! I understand!' Carly said it automatically.

'Then I can tell the family that,' on the other end of the line, the lawyer paused again, thinking of some euphemism for the crudity of legal action, '. . . that you will not be taking any steps to reverse the situation?'

In other words, that she would not sue for what she had lost through the cancellation of her Broadway opening.

'Yes!' Carly said abruptly. 'Yes, you can tell them that!'

The conversation was on tape. She hadn't heard the click as the recording device went on but, in that moment, Carly knew it. The Calthrops did not believe in taking chances.

'Yes!' If they wanted evidence they could take into any court, then they could have it. 'Yes,' Carly repeated clearly, 'you can tell the family that I want and expect nothing from either them or Mr Calthrop. The only thing I ask is that they let me know how Mr Calthrop is progressing!'

Her receiver was already on its way back to the cradle before the Boston lawyer had even started to reply.

So, that was it! Carly stood and surveyed the luxury of her suite and saw nothing. She was on her own again; back once more where she had been at the beginning.

She was surprised to find someone behind her when she finally turned away from the telephone. It was generally enough for room service to leave the bill. After twelve—No! Almost thirteen weeks' residence in that particular suite—it was enough for them to leave the check and have her sign it with the Calthrop name, but this must be a new man to whom the routine was unfamiliar.

At first she looked no further than a pair of well-shaped hands, looking for the bill and ballpoint pen, then she looked behind him for the trolley. It was only then, seeing none of those particular things, that she finally looked up at the man himself.

'Hallo, Charlotte!'

Beyond the big french windows leading to the terrace with its potted plants and shrubs, life in San Francisco must have carried on as normal. Here, however, in this quiet suite fifteen storeys above the ground, it stopped absolutely dead.

'You seem surprised!' Words in that so familiar voice came from a great distance.

'Yes!' She let out her breath. 'I thought you were room service!' Things began to move again; curtains blowing in from the windows, the ticking of a clock.

'Really?' A half smile like a crooked question mark glinted on a lean, sardonic face. 'In that case, I must apologise! I have no doubt tea would have been more welcome, or——' the smile grew mocking under steady, level eyes, '——is it coffee now that you're so thoroughly Americanised?'

Blood began to circulate and her heartbeat

settled down. 'Neither!' Carly said shortly. 'I don't drink tea or coffee in the afternoon! What are you doing here——?' She stopped. 'What are you doing here, Daniel?'

The sound of his name in her voice after so many years finally made the situation real. It *was* Daniel standing there in front of her, feet apart, weight balanced easily as he stood and watched her above the characteristic irony of his crooked smile.

His hair was grey! She realised it with a sense of shock. At first, she thought he hadn't changed but there were grey hairs at the temples and above the ears in the thick mane which, when she had last seen it, had been jet black. There were wrinkles, too, in tiny fans at the corner of his narrowed eyes and perhaps the years had etched the lines between his nose and mouth a little deeper. For most men, this would have been an alarming sign of their mortality but for Daniel—Daniel Stone—grey hair and the outward signs of time passing only served to emphasise the strength of intellect and purpose that made him not just striking but—Carly shivered—overwhelming.

'What do you want?' She broke the little silence curtly.

'To see you!' If anything, her defensiveness only left him more amused.

She nodded pointedly towards the door. 'Well, now you've seen me, I suggest you leave!'

Daniel didn't move.

'I can always call Security!' she threatened.

'Indeed you can!' He studied her with easy confidence. 'But somehow I don't think you will!'

'Really?' She tried for haughtiness. 'Then just stay exactly where you are for another fifteen seconds and you can find out just how wrong you are!' She reached for the telephone, only to have it taken from her and replaced on its cradle. 'I warn you, Daniel . . .!'

She might as well have tried to threaten the floor beneath his feet.

'You know,' he mused, 'you haven't changed! How long is it? Eight years? Nine?' He couldn't even remember the date of their divorce! 'And to see you now——' the inspection of slate grey eyes made her acutely uncomfortable, '—it could have been yesterday!'

'Unfortunately for you, it isn't!' Carly moved out of the direct rays of the sunlight pouring through the open window. 'What do you want, Daniel? Tell me and then get out!'

'What do I want?' Not in the least abashed, he went on studying her. 'What I want is very simple. I want you!'

A fist hit her squarely in the chest and the room and Daniel blurred and wavered to and fro. 'You're crazy!' she said thickly.

'Probably!' His voice came to her from a long way off. 'My problem is, I don't seem to have any choice!'

Daniel Stone! Stage director at twenty-two; overall producer and one of the most sought after men in the English theatre a year later. Brilliant! A prodigy!

She hadn't known him then, of course. She had still been in some army base high school—probably in the Middle East—sublimely and supremely unaware of everything except a burning, naively ignorant ambition to be an actress and then a star.

She had met Daniel at her second West End mass audition. One of forty or fifty unknown faces, neither luck nor talent had won a part for her, even as a non-speaking extra, but fluke had had her at the stage door when Daniel left. She had lost her purse with all the money she possessed to see her through the month and she had backtracked everywhere she had been that day in the desperate hope that someone had returned it.

Daniel had been slimmer then. No! Not slimmer. He had still had a trace of the boyishness which had since hardened and refined into the taut, hard outline of the man now facing her. But the sharp incision of the jaw had been there even then and the quiet assessment of the eyes—grey when happy and a chilling, glinting slate when not.

'You're crazy!' She repeated it somewhere in the direction of his throat where the tanned skin disappeared beneath the brilliant white contrast of his open necked shirt. 'We're finished, Daniel! Over! There's no more wanting left!'

She could remember the texture of the skin underneath that shirt. Hard and warm as she had run her fingers over it, tracing the outline of the bone and muscle of his chest until his mouth had captured hers and her hands had been trapped and held against the pillows on either side of her head.

Now, though, the shirt was tucked in at the waist and a broad belt held the faded jeans snugly at his hips. No one except Daniel would have gained entry to this particular hotel dressed like that: no one except Daniel would have been allowed past the door, far less been permitted unannounced access to her suite.

'Perhaps, on your side, everything *is* over!' Daniel drawled. 'Unfortunately, that doesn't seem to be the case on mine!'

Her throat went dry and the words hurt as she got them out. 'Don't, Daniel! There's no point! Please!' She heard the pleading note and bitterly resented it. 'Go away!'

He heard it, too, and it put a glint of victory in his smile as he crossed the room. 'Not until I've told you why I'm here!'

'I don't want to know!' She turned away only to have his fingers in the hollows of her shoulders turn her back. Her whole body leaped, then stiffened. 'Please, Daniel! Whatever it is, I don't want to know!'

'But you're going to!' He was insistent. 'You might even be pleased when you hear what I've got to say!'

'I doubt it!' She pulled her shoulders from his hands and walked to a safe distance. 'I doubt very much that anything you say could even *interest* me!'

'But you'll listen?'

She looked at him, standing between her and

the door. 'It doesn't seem as if I've got much choice, does it?'

'No,' he said, 'it doesn't!'

'Then say what you've got to say and get out!' she snapped. 'I've got to be at the . . .!' Her voice trailed away. 'I've got to be at the theatre in an hour! It had almost automatically slipped out. But that was no longer true. There was no theatre—nothing!—now that Bram was no longer there. This hotel suite was hers for a few more days and then it was back to New York and more auditions. A little better off, maybe, then she had been when she had left. At least, now, she had her San Francisco notices but although notices might get her some attention and respect—an agent from the William Morris agency had already called up with a view to setting up a meeting to see if the firm could represent her—but there was bound to be a long delay before other work came along to fill the void that Bram's departure had left in her life.

Spinning out the moment deliberately to torment her, Daniel picked up a small, ceramic figure of a dancer from the table beside the window. Bram had bought it for her. She had seen it in one of the big waterfront art galleries and immediately fallen in love with it. Never likely to have any great commercial or investment value, it nevertheless had a sense of grace and movement that had immediately appealed to her.

'Nice!' Daniel approved. 'Is it yours, or does it come with the bridal suite!' Above the little dancer, he looked around the plush and gilt with obvious amusement.

'It's mine!' Carly was short. 'Get on with it, Daniel! What have you got to say?'

He replaced the figure carefully on the glass topped table. 'Nothing much,' he straightened. 'Just a proposal!' Her throat closed up again. 'I've got a season starting up in Canada,' he said dispassionately. 'You may have heard of it? Theatre on the Lake!' He paused, head on one side, watching her. 'No? I thought you might! In that case, then, you'll hardly know that my female lead's dropped out. That's why I'm here. I'd be grateful if you would take her place!'

'Oh! I see!' Carly's heart decelerated from its impossibly fast pace. What had she thought he was going to propose? Marriage? 'And you've come all this way just to ask me that?'

'Not *just* to ask you that, Charlotte!' For a moment, Daniel sounded tired. 'Not unless you consider the future of an entire theatrical season something not worth the bother of a journey! Without Margaret, we're going to be in trouble!' There was no tiredness now, either in the voice or in the sharp, abrasive look. 'I've got a new play slated, we're reviving a Pinero and, in slightly more than four weeks' time, we're due to open with *The Seagull!*'

'And you want me to play *Nina*?' All actress now, Carly was totally disbelieving. She had once seen Vanessa Redgrave in the part—it must have been during one of her father's leaves when they were in London—and playing it had become a goal, almost an obsession. If she could interpret

Chekhov's Nina to that standard, she would know that her faith in herself as an actress had been justified.

'Yes!' Daniel was absolutely serious.

'And you think I can?' Carly felt her own excitement. 'I mean, you don't think I'm too old or too inexperienced?'

'Too old?' Daniel paused and studied her, head on one side. 'No, I don't think so!'

For once, his scrutiny of her face and figure failed to bother her. It was clinical, dispassionate; a top flight director appraising not the woman who had once been his wife but the actress—the performer—who would be behind the footlights taking the audience with her into Chekhov's nineteenth century Russian world.

To him, the wide clear mouth, the excited flashing eyes were no more than properties, tools of her trade. As for her figure—the long legs, flat hips and stomach and softly rounded breasts—if it was necessary, she could always lose some weight. Not that she really needed to. At almost thirty diet and a fixation about working out—often involuntary diet in the past when work had failed to materialise—had kept her measurements much the same as they had been when she was nineteen.

If there had been children, it might have been different—for a moment, Daniel's inspection seemed less than clinical—but when she had walked out on Daniel, she had walked out without ties of any kind.

'And you don't think I'm too inexperienced?'

She had no idea why she had to remind him of her shortcomings for a part she would gladly give a year of her life to play. It could only be to fill the silence as his eyes ranged over her and stopped once more, abruptly, on her face.

'I doubt it!' His voice was dry. 'I've seen your notices. What was it they said? The north American theatre's new, young Geraldine Page!'

His smile took away her sudden wave of pleasure that he had cared at least enough about her as an actress to read her notices.

'I'm sorry it's so hard for you to believe!' She said belligerently.

'Not hard but ... Oh!' Beneath the newly greying hair his interest died. 'Never mind the word! I'll take it as read that you're as good as they say you are!'

'Thank you!' she said thinly.

'Not at all!' He inclined his head above mocking eyes. 'And even if you're not,' it was not a threat or warning but something in between, 'you will be by the time we've finished rehearsals and the curtain goes up on opening night!'

'Oh!' She coloured, feeling foolish.

'Incidentally,' Daniel changed the subject with one of his sudden swerves, 'there is something I have been meaning to ask you!'

'What?' Her head jolted back, bringing her face to face with him.

'Why you changed your name to Carly,' he said smoothly. 'What happened to the Charlotte Mason I once knew?'

'Nothing happened!' She was just a little older,

a little more in control. Ten years ago, seeing Daniel watching her like that would have sent her pulse rate soaring and her heart fluttering like a bird in a cage. 'Carly just seemed more suitable, that was all!'

Marketable, in fact, had been the word Bram's go-getting account executive had used. When he had taken over the running of her career, Bram had done it with all the thoroughness of a manufacturer launching a new product. Using the resources of the Calthrop family interests, opinions had been sought and research done and Charlotte, the consensus was, had conjured up an image of someone stuffy and middle-aged.

Fine if you were going to settle down and write Gothic novels like Charlotte Brontë, the young account exec. had pointed out, but not if you were going to take the theatre world by storm.

Settling on a new name had led to endless talk going, sometimes, far on into the night. 'Rap sessions', as they were called by the young account executive who seemed, to Carly, to live in a vocabulary all his own.

Charlie! was already identified with the perfume and she, herself, had been adamant about a complete change so Charlotte had become Carly and she had already become so used to it that it came almost as a shock to hear her old name on Daniel's lips.

She pushed a sudden shivery reaction to one side. 'You know—new life, new image!' she said defensively. 'Besides,' she too could also change the subject, 'you haven't told me how you knew where to find me!'

'And you haven't been listening!' Daniel drawled. 'I read your notices, remember?'

'Oh, yes! I see!' To escape from him, she looked around the room. It should have changed since Daniel had come in but it was just the same. Dove grey carpet wall to wall; drapes blowing in from the french windows leading to the balcony and a view of San Francisco's pink tiled roof tops going right down to the Bay. 'I didn't think you'd bother!'

'Just as you no longer bother to read *Variety* or *Stage*?' He glanced at the week's editions of the show business papers on the table beside the Empire couch.

'No!' She smiled and, for a moment, she forgot. For just a moment, she was back ten years, sitting up in bed, naked to the waist, with Daniel similarly dressed beside her.

She had been laughing, her long brown hair wild about her face. 'Mine!' She had reached down and grabbed the paper from the bedspread and held it away from him.

'No! Mine!' Daniel also had been laughing, his teeth white against the natural tan of his face and his hair, too, rumpled from the pillow. He had reached across to get the paper from her hand and, as he did so, his arm had brushed against her breast. Everything had stopped as he looked down at her and later, much, much later, she had picked the paper up from the floor beside the bed.

That had been in their flat in London and—her heart contracted—Daniel hadn't really changed. The hair might be greying, cut a little shorter and worn in a different style—thick and full and brushed across his forehead in a dense sweep above his brows—but the particular image she had somehow carried in her heart had been stamped there ten long years before. Besides—she made an effort to be rational—everything was different now. Fashions—everything—had changed since then. And something else had, too.

Then, Daniel had been the one so much in demand. Charlotte Mason—Mrs Stone—had been no more than an adjunct to the great Daniel Stone. Someone whose insistence on a career in her own right had increasingly become the cause of destructive, frightening arguments.

But now *she* had succeeded. Her determination had been justified. She might have been forced to leave her marriage, leave her home and come to America to do it but, at last, she had proved that her faith in herself had been warranted.

'You can do it!' Daniel was once more talking about the part he was offering her. 'The point is——' he held her levelly with his eyes, '—will you?'

Daniel was here and Daniel was asking her. She just wished triumph had a sweeter taste.

'I've got a production starting in four weeks!' He listed facts and figures. 'I've got three more plays to get ready for the season and then, last week, I'm told that one of my leading actresses is dropping out! It's all there!' He nodded towards the two trade papers.

Yes, she knew it was. She might choose not to admit it but both the American *Variety* and the British *Stage* had carried features on Daniel Stone's new project and she had read them.

Theatre on a Northern Lake had been one heading. Daniel was taking the best of Stratford, Niagara and Halifax's Neptune Theatre to the shores of Lake Ontario and starting a whole new concept of drama in Canada. The stories had started several months ago when the appointment of an Englishman to direct in the Canadian theatre had caused a furore that had gone as far as Ottawa with a prime minister answering questions in parliament about why Daniel Stone was considered so indispensable.

Somehow a compromise had been reached. Daniel Stone was to direct the first season and get the project off the ground. After that? It had seemed to Carly that the future had been left deliberately vague.

To her, the whole issue had been of only the most academic interest. At least, that was what she had struggled to convince herself when Daniel's picture had first leaped out at her from the grainy pages. Daniel was a part of her past life. The present was now—and Bram—and the play that had then been in the planning stages for San Francisco. There was no need for her stomach to feel hollow and her breath like something hard and painful in her throat.

Now, however, Daniel was watching her and

the story that had been of only academic interest was in the room.

'Why me? I mean . . .!' Carly gestured with her hands. 'I know you've read my notices but there must be a lot of other actresses who could take Margaret's place!'

She had given herself away and she saw him smile. The story about Margaret Duboisson's withdrawal had been a stop press item in that week's *Variety* at the foot of the back page. If she had seen it, her interest in and knowledge of his project was obvious.

'Of course!' He didn't bother to hide his confidence. 'There are—a lot! The only problem is—they're not Canadian!'

'And I am!' She had never been more mortified and angry in her life. A Canadian father and a mother born in the heartland of the United States; what she had always considered an advantage now brought angry colour rushing to her cheeks. No matter how much immigration restrictions tightened, she could still live and work in both countries and in England where, by chance, she had been born. And that was her attraction! That was why Daniel had bothered to seek her out. Not for her talent or her skill but because of her triple nationality.

He considered her angry face with a slow smile. 'Not quite one hundred per cent Canadian,' he said, 'but good enough!'

'And you think that just because I can save your precious production from disaster, I'm going to leave everything I've got going for me here and work for you?' She was so furious she could hardly speak.

'I hardly thought you had too much to leave!' Daniel pointed out. 'I read the papers, too, you know!'

And those particular papers had had stories about her and Bram. A tussle between a rarely heard of Boston family and an actress now facing the cancellation of her Broadway debut because her 'backer'—no one had been more suggestive about their relationship than that—had been seriously injured in a road accident. That little snippet of pure soap opera plot had certainly been enough to make the gossip columns.

'I hate you, Daniel!' She turned away, facing the window now and the blood red sun sinking across the Bay.

'Maybe!' His voice reached out and touched her through the shadows and a tremor went down her spine. 'But I still think you'll come! *Nina!* Remember, Charlotte? The part you've always wanted to play! Call me tomorrow and let me know!' His footsteps went away across the carpet and then stopped. 'Incidentally,' he must be beside the door, 'there is one thing I should tell you. There will be no special treatment just because you were once my wife!'

CHAPTER THREE

THEATRES did not run themselves. They needed box office staff and caterers; front and back of house management; stage door keepers and part and fulltime cleaners; programme sellers and gardeners. Then there were the electricians and the carpenters but they were somewhere near the top of the huge interdependent pyramid of people necessary to operate an enterprise of the size and magnitude of Theatre on the Lake. Carpenters and electricians actually had contact with the raked, almost circular apron stage which projected far out into the elegant red plush comfort of the auditorium. They built the sets and controlled the lights necessary to take that most important group of all—the audience—into the dramatic world of fantasy and make-believe which all this skilled and concentrated effort was designed to achieve.

And above the tradesmen and their skills were more people still. The actors; a group of widely differing individuals drawn from all over Canada and, above them, quite alone at the top of this vast pyramid of different personalities and skills there was one man, the artistic director. The man who had complete control over everything. There was Daniel Stone.

'Right, Charlotte! Back to that last move where

Ed comes across to you and, this time,' behind the lights, coming from somewhere in the darkened auditorium, Daniel's voice was tired, 'try and put some heart in it. You're a girl, Charlotte, a young, impressionable girl and Moscow, in the person of Trigorin, has just been presented to you as being within your grasp. It's a world you've always longed for. A world of art and life and love and you're glowing, soaring at the thought it could be yours. Okay, then,' weariness which had disappeared as he opened up the motivation behind the lines she spoke, once more returned to Daniel's voice, 'let's go back and take it from Trigorin's cross.'

Trigorin's footsteps came across the stage and Carly poised herself. Heart, Daniel had said. Well, she would give him heart. She would ignore the fact that Ed McMaster's suddenly attainable Trigorin suffered from bad breath and she would give Daniel what he wanted if she died in the attempt.

Taking the breath that would last her through her first line, she turned towards Trigorin.

'Not bad!' Two hours later, Carly was shivering and exhausted and Daniel's voice had changed. Now it was grudging. 'I guess we might as well call it a day. We've time enough before the first public dress rehearsal, especially as it now seems there's a chance we'll have things in some sort of shape! Notes in the morning, ladies and gentlemen!' He stopped the general onstage drift in the direction of the exits. 'At nine-thirty!' he added over the universal groan.

This time, the cast disappeared with Carly following them but, 'Charlotte!' In the darkness of the auditorium, she heard Daniel's assistant and secretary get up and leave and Daniel walk down the centre aisle towards her.

'Yes, what is it?' She drew her shawl more closely round her shoulders and turned to face him.

It was a rehearsal shawl, supplied by wardrobe to give her a feeling of the period. Later there would be the full costume for which she had stood for so many hours through so many fittings but, for now, Chekhov's Nina with her dark hair pulled back from her face and secured with a rubber band, was wearing tights and leg warmers with canvas running shoes and a baggy man-sized sweater which, even with the somewhat threadbare shawl, did not seem able to stop her shaking.

'Hard luck!' One of the other actresses passing on her way out commiserated in a whisper. 'We'll see you later! And remember——' she paused for a fraction of a second, 'he's really only a friendly ogre!'

They loved him. To them he was a god. This Englishman who had the power to make or break their working lives. He could shout, scream, rage—No! That wasn't fair. Daniel never quite did that. He got angry, maybe, frustrated when people couldn't grasp the finer points of his dramatic interpretation but, once the first outburst of explosive anger had run its course, the result was always endless patience, helping towards a performance which even the most experienced of actors in the company had not dreamed they were capable of giving.

And for that, they worshipped him. *The* great Daniel Stone. Brilliant, autocratic, in complete command of this particular pyramid. Emperor Stone!

'Yes,' Carly repeated coldly, 'what is it you want?'

He appeared from the gloom of the empty auditorium and, for a moment, standing under the harsh stage working lights and looking down at him, Carly almost weakened; felt something of the near idolatry in which the others, even the self important Ed McMaster, clearly held him. It was an emotion dangerously close to the one which had consumed her all those years earlier. Love!

'Here!' Daniel looked tired as he walked slowly down towards her. The stride was there and the easy movement but weariness had etched the lines more deeply on his face and the burden of responsibility for the entire season was visible on his shoulders. For once, the grey hair did not seem so shocking or the glasses which he now took off and folded and slipped into the breast pocket of his black shirt.

If she was nudging thirty, then Daniel must be almost forty; almost twice the age she had been when she had walked out on their marriage.

Their marriage! By this time, Daniel had walked into the area of the stage lights and all illusion of tiredness promptly vanished along with any last vestige of compassion.

'Come down here and sit down!' A hand came up to help her off the stage. 'I want to talk to you!'

She didn't move. 'I'd rather stay here, thank you!'

His lips compressed in a narrow line. 'As you wish!' He turned away, took an end seat in the second row of stalls and put his feet up on the back of the seat in front of him, leaving her standing there, totally exposed and somehow foolish on the empty stage. 'Robin tells me you and he have been having problems!' He began without preamble.

Robin Thurgood was the company's press and public relations manager.

'Not that I know of!' Carly shrugged. Looking down at him, she felt not just ridiculous but far too aware of the easy length of body stretched between the seats.

At this angle and in the lights, the grey hair had vanished. He was dark and tough and powerful with piercing grey eyes boring into her; the Daniel she had met all those years earlier when she had gone back to a stage door in desperate search of a missing purse and Daniel had come through and seen her and offered her a ride home in his taxi.

'Then Robin must have been mistaken,' he said quietly. 'He's got some curious idea that you're unhappy with your billing!'

'Not my billing!' She at once over-reacted. 'Robin's using my wrong name!'

'Really?' If anything, he grew even more

relaxed, crossing his arms and shifting to a more comfortable position as he regarded her above the narrow question mark of his smile. 'I've always thought Charlotte Mason was quite a pleasant name. And presumably—you do, too. At least,' he smile broadened but the eyes stayed just the same, 'you certainly lost no time in going back to it when you stopped being Mrs Daniel Stone!'

'Dammit, Daniel!' His reference to their marriage made her angry and ill at ease. 'You know exactly what I mean! I told you when I called you!' The next morning in San Francisco, in his hotel, to accept his offer for this season, just as he had known she would. '*You* don't want anyone to know about our marriage and *I* want to be known as Carly Mason on everything that goes out of here. What's the point of getting somewhere with my career at last—of getting all those notices,' she unconsciously held out an imaginary fistful of her notices from the San Francisco papers, 'if I'm not going to be allowed to capitalise on what I've achieved so far? I've worked for what I've got, Daniel,' she almost choked, 'worked—and starved and no one knows who Charlotte Mason is and no one could care less. I don't give a damn where my name comes on the billing——' the billing, in fact, was alphabetical, '—but I do care very much which name is used. That's what I told Robin! I am not—not!' she repeated fiercely, 'going back to being an unknown!'

She might just as well have saved her breath.

From his lazily relaxed position, Daniel looked

up at her. 'Two points,' he said quite calmly. 'Firstly, however much you might wish you could deny the fact, the notices of which you are so proud were bought and guaranteed by a totally infatuated man! And secondly,' he over-rode the beginnings of her explosive protest, 'Carly is *not* your name! It is the end product of a slick piece of public relations work designed to give you mass appeal!'

It was. At least, it was the product of the resources on which the shadowy Calthrop enterprises could draw when they wanted to sound out a market. Carly! She could remember the young account executive rolling it around his tongue like some fine old wine. The world of serious theatre was just panting for a Carly!

'And as this theatre aims to offer something a little more substantial than slick mass appeal,' Daniel continued in the same icy tone of voice, 'you will be known as Charlotte Mason on every scrap of printed matter and publicity material Robin puts out of here. I have no intention of allowing your ambition to associate *my* theatre with Calthrop's sort of operation in any way, shape or form. I paid you the compliment of offering you this season because I thought you might—just might—have reached the point where you could do it. But here, you stand or fall on the strength of your own talent, not on the cushion of the Calthrop milions!'

'Is that all?' Carly was sullen. How dare he speak to her like that?

'Yes,' he said, 'that's all. Goodnight, Charlotte!

And incidentally,' in the act of getting smoothly to his feet, his eyes passed briefly across her face, 'you're looking tired! If you're sensible, you'll get an early night!'

She waited, all alone on an empty stage, until even the sound of his footsteps had died away, and then, in a sudden spasm of useless rage, she ripped off the inoffensive rehearsal shawl and flung it after him.

'Finished, miss?' Upstage, beside the flat, the electrician responsible for switching off the working lights was watching her.

'What?' He had startled her.

'I was wondering if you'd finished for the night?'

'Oh, yes! Yes, I have!' With any luck, he had only just arrived and would think her temper tantrum was part of some out of hours rehearsal she had stayed on late to give herself. She didn't think she could bear it if anyone had overheard what Daniel had just said to her. And yet, in the act of stepping across the footlights and scrambling down from the stage to retrieve the much abused shawl, Carly paused.

In pulling down her dream world and exposing the real truth behind her success, Daniel might have said a little more than he intended. He had flown all the way to San Francisco to offer her *this* season in *this* theatre beside the lake because her Canadian citizenship posed fewer problems in his search for a replacement for the actress who had dropped out. That was what he had told her.

She could see him now, standing in her hotel

suite with the curtains blowing in behind him at the windows, making the reason for his choice extremely plain. And yet, just a few minutes earlier, not in a hotel suite but sitting in that seat—Carly looked at the red plush velvet—with his feet up on the one in front of it, he had said that he had asked her not because of any citizenship but because he thought she could play the part.

Carly stooped and picked up the shawl. Daniel had said that she had talent! Stars shone in the empty, darkened roof and, behind her, on the stage, the electrician's tuneless whistling was the Emperor's nightingale.

Daniel thought that she could act.

Euphoria about this unintentional compliment took her out of the theatre and through the town towards the rented house she shared.

The theatre had been grafted on to a little lakeshore town founded by some of the United Empire Loyalists who had come north to stay under the British flag when the original thirteen American colonies had declared their independence from the Crown. On the surface, nothing much about the town had changed since the arrival of those high-minded refugees across the border of what had then been Upper Canada some two hundred years before. White clapboard houses—some little more than cottages, some much larger with graceful, cool verandahs and every indication that their builders had been men of wealth and substance—lined the very wide central thoroughfare and went back two or three

blocks on either side. The more modern part of
town—what there was of it—was a mile or so
away, out of sight and out of mind.

It was blossom time; peach and cherry and
flowering tulip trees half hid the immaculate
white houses with their shingled roofs. In the
fresh warmth of the late spring evening, the air
was scented, heady.

People here took a pride in their surroundings.
That was why the one and only garage on Main
Street had been made to set its signs well back in
its forecourt so that the visitor's first impression
was of a vista of unchanged, Colonial charm.

The cars, though, gave the game away. The
most rigorous of city fathers could do nothing
about them and, even this early in the season and
this late in the day, some were still parked at an
angle along either side of the central, tree lined
boulevard and more were along the kerbs. Seeing
those cars, Carly felt a flutter of nervous
excitement in her stomach.

In a few weeks' time there would be even more
and their owners would be sitting, watching her,
in the theatre.

Carly walked through the front gate into her
own garden and stopped when she saw who was
sitting on the verandah.

'I should pour that can of beer over your head!'
she said half seriously. 'What did you have to go
to Daniel for?'

She shared a house with two of the other
girls—one in wardrobe, the other apprenticing
in stage design. She had been lucky, really.

Lodgings in the town were at a premium. The arrival of the theatre had been greeted with mixed feelings and some resistance, not many residents were prepared to rent accommodation to the invaders, and Carly had slipped into what could have well been the last space.

A little narrow room in the attic of a little narrow house overlooking Main Street and the garage with its despised signs.

However, three girls sharing inevitably attracted visitors. There was always someone there, either in the tiny parlour or stretched out comfortably on one of the old cane chairs on the verandah and this evening, it was Robin Thurgood, the press and public relations man.

'Yes, sorry about that!' Robin had obviously heard the news that she had been kept back for a roasting and knew the reason. 'But you did come on a bit strong, you know, when I tried to talk to you! What else was I to do except go to Daniel?' He raised a languid arm and waved a can of beer apologetically in her direction.

She liked Robin. With his weakness for two-inch Cuban heels, tightly fitting pants and brightly coloured satin shirts, she had at first thought him effeminate but first impressions had quickly changed when she had been coming down the stairs early one morning and almost bumped into him coming out of Cindy's room. He was nice and bright and young and fun and, even if he had gone and complained to Daniel, she would forgive anyone anything for that admission, unwitting though it might have been, that, at long last, Daniel considered she could act.

Surely it wasn't dangerous that one thing should mean so much?

'Anyway,' Robin cut through the disconcerting little thought, 'what's it going to be? Charlotte or Carly?'

'Charlotte!' She coloured. 'Why even ask when I'm sure you've already guessed! From now on, I'm to be Charlotte Mason on every bit of paper and scrap of publicity you put out!'

'In that case,' Robin raised his can of beer and studied her amiably across the rim, 'Hi, Charlotte! Come and have a drink!' He reached down into the shade underneath his chair and produced another can from the six pack he had brought.

'Oh, no! No, thanks! I'd better go inside and learn a few more lines!' She was already studying the part of Trelawney for the second play of the season. 'And incidentally, Robin!' She stopped in the open doorway leading from the verandah into the back kitchen. 'It's only Charlotte for publicity. For the rest of the time, I'm still Carly!'

Daniel wasn't going to have a total victory.

She was in her room, trying to concentrate on lines when she heard Cindy and Angela come back. Cindy and Angela back from a late night opening shopping trip with that week's groceries, judging from the fact that Robin seemed to have come in from the verandah and all the noise and talking was coming from the kitchen two floors below her room.

In the general division of responsibility that went with sharing accommodation, Carly had done rather well, she thought. All the day to day bills for such things as grocery and laundry were to be shared equally but, for a little more than Carly's third share of the rent, Cindy and Angela were willing to do all the cooking and the shopping.

The rationale was that as well as working all day in the theatre—all day and then often late into the evening or whatever time it was Daniel decided to call a halt—Carly also had lines to learn in what was laughingly called her spare time. Actually, she suspected, both Cindy and Angela were grateful to have their share of the rent reduced. Angela was still an apprentice in stage design and Cindy was only in her first season as a seamstress-cum-assistant in the wardrobe department.

Wages in out of town theatre—particularly new theatre and particularly theatre in which Daniel Stone had any sort of hand—were hardly generous. After what she had been getting in San Francisco, Carly had hardly been able to believe what Daniel had offered her.

It hadn't been quite 'take it or leave it!': nor had it quite been that the small amount was only what he considered she was worth but, 'It's more than Actor's Guild minimum,' he had said over the telephone from his hotel. 'And that's only for the actual season. Rehearsal rates will be less, of course!'

He had already made the point that he would

not be paying expenses for her flight to Canada from San Francisco—no leisurely drive back now with Bram, stopping at luxury hotels en route. And no repaying Bram for all he had done for her.

'You can have your agent call me and discuss it, if you like,' Daniel had cut through a stupendous feeling of almost lightheaded relief, 'but what I've offered you is as far as I can go!'

Her agent! She didn't have an agent. Bram had taken care of that side of her career. Until now— until the call from William Morris a few days earlier—none of the worthwhile agents had even been interested in representing her.

'No, that's all right!' Carly had said it quickly—too quickly for her peace of mind. 'There's no need to do that! I accept!'

'In that case, I'll drop a contract off at your hotel on my way to the airport and get the bell captain to bring it up to you,' Daniel had said. 'Sign it and bring it when you come!'

She wasn't even worth his while to stop off and deliver it himself, Carly had thought as she replaced the telephone.

But at least she could subsidise herself with what she had earned in San Francisco while she was here. Lying on the narrow bed, chin cupped in her hands and script propped up in front of her on the pillow, Cary heard the sounds of supper being got ready in the kitchen down below and felt a twinge of guilt. But why should she be feeling guilty? She was paying and, besides, Cindy and Angela liked cooking, whereas she never had.

Anything that had got in the way of her career had not been worth bothering with.

'Bloody tins!' She remembered one of the many occasions when Daniel had sat glowering at one of her scratch meals, jet black head bent aggressively towards her as he had looked down at the table of their London flat and inspected that evening's offering of spaghetti and meat balls. 'Is it too much to ask that sometimes—just sometimes—you should go out and buy something that you can cook yourself?' he demanded angrily.

'I'm sorry!' Carly felt her temper rise. 'But I happen to have been auditioning all day!'

'Auditioning?' Daniel was thin. 'Or hanging around in coffee bars gossiping with all those out of work layabouts you call your friends!'

'They are not layabouts—they are actors, talented people, just like me!' Carly had responded furiously. 'Besides, how else am I going to get to know what's happening? *You* won't tell me anything! You'd think being married to the great Daniel Stone would be an advantage to my career, not a liability! Anyway,' she switched tacks, 'it wouldn't hurt you to cook supper occasionally!'

'On a primus stove, on stage while I'm working, I suppose!' Daniel snapped. 'And what do I do then? Put it in a hay box to keep warm until I can bring it home? Come on, darling,' he was holding out an olive branch, 'we've been through all this so many times before. You know I don't believe in patronage! If you've got what it takes, you're going to make it and you're going to make it on your own. All I'm asking is that, until you do, I get a home-cooked meal occasionally!'

She wasn't being fair, she wasn't! Daniel did cook sometimes; Daniel did encourage her. It was just that he was as adamant about not using his position to help her in any way as she was determined not to let him see she knew she was in the wrong.

'And after all those home-cooked meals, it'll be children, I suppose!' she said belligerently.

'And what's wrong with that!' Daniel stopped trying to patch things over and anger put a white line around his lips. 'What's wrong with wanting a family, for God's sake! You've so much time, Charlotte! How often do I have to tell you that? It'll be ten years—maybe more—before you even come close to reaching your full potential as an actress. By that time we can have a couple of kids—one, if you like—they'll be at school, we can have help, anything you want, and you'll be free to pick up your career!'

'When I'm middle aged with a waistline like an elephant's and no one's got a clue either who I am or what I've done!' From the vantage point of twenty, thirty seemed a long way off. Not that thirty seemed to have done Daniel any harm. The muscles of the chest were flat and hard as he leaned towards her across the table and authority had stamped the darkly handsome face, not age. If she aged half as well, she would be a striking woman—maybe even beautiful—in ten years' time and Daniel could well be right in saying that what she was now trying so hard to achieve would, of its own volition, fall into her hands. But she wanted what she wanted now!

'How very generous,' she said acidly. 'You get your own way and I wait and take my chance. Thanks, Daniel, but no thanks. Now, eat your spaghetti!' She picked up her own fork. 'Because it's all you're going to get!'

Daniel had got up then and slammed out of the flat and she had slept alone that night for the first time in their married life.

They had made it up, of course, just as they always made up their arguments, with Daniel's body fitting against her own as if it had been specially made for it. But finally, the rifts grew deeper, the arguments more difficult to forget until, one Sunday evening, she had been the one who had slammed out of that London flat.

In the narrow house, three thousand miles and thousands more days away from that traumatic evening, Carly found herself reading and re-reading the same line in her script. She rolled over on the bed and swung her feet down on to the floor. She was thinking much too much about the past. She was also thinking much too much about Daniel Stone. What she needed was a break from studying her lines and some company.

'Hi! I was just going to come up and call you!' At the stove, Angela turned and grinned across her shoulder as Carly walked in through the kitchen door. 'Food's ready——' Angela scooped a hissing saucepan from the ring and carried it to the sink, '—or just about!'

'It smells good, anyway!' Carly watched plump, blonde Angela half disappear in a cloud of steam. 'Is there anything I can do? Lay the table?'

'No!' Busy with her potato masher, Angela once more grinned. 'Cindy and Robin are supposed to be doing that! Can't you hear!'

Laughter and voices were coming from the dining room and Carly heard Cindy's high-pitched squeal as Robin, presumably, said—or did—something typically outrageous.

She frowned. 'So Robin's staying to eat with us, is he?'

'Yes—but it's okay!' Angela rushed to reassure her. 'Cindy'll pay his share!'

'Oh, for God's sake, Angela!' Something snapped. 'That wasn't what I meant!' Now just why was it that she was so annoyed? 'I'm sorry,' Carly tried to make amends, 'I must be tired, that's all!'

'That's okay! Who isn't tired? But,' Angela turned away and went on with her mashing, 'there is something you could do, if you don't mind. You could take the salad through!'

All through dinner, Angela kept shooting her the odd, speculative look. She had forgiven but she couldn't quite forget. Perhaps having *Charlotte* Mason to share with them *had* been a mistake. She was, after all, quite a lot older and now she was behaving as if she were a star.

'Oh, Carly!' Not involved, Cindy suddenly looked up half way through dessert. 'Did you get your message?'

'No? What message?' For no particular reason, Carly's heartbeat speeded up.

'I left it on the table in the hall,' Cindy explained. 'A phone message. I should have told you, I suppose.' Carly's heartbeat changed to a fast thump. No one except Daniel knew that she was there. 'A man called Calthorpe. He left a number for you to call him—somewhere in the States.'

'It's Calthrop,' Carly corrected sharply. 'And don't worry, I'll use my credit card to make the call but—thanks, Cindy!' Now Cindy was looking slightly hurt. It was one of those evenings when when nothing was going right. 'Thanks for taking the message, anyway!'

It was hardly Cindy's fault that it was Bram who called. Going towards the telephone, Carly felt guilty on two counts. First because of Cindy and then because of Bram. How long was it since she had given Bram more than a passing thought? Once he had been not just part but all of her everyday life but, since the day she had stood on the airport apron at San Francisco and watched the doors of the private Calthrop family jet close behind his stretcher, Bram had seemed to belong to another world.

She knew he was recovering from his accident. By the time the hydraulic door of the private Calthrop family jet had hissed shut, he was already sufficiently well on his way for the doctors to be able to predict that there would be no long-lasting after effects. And she had called Boston once or twice; the last time had been the evening she arrived here, in this house. But then rehearsals had claimed her—she refused to allow her mind to be less general about the reason for her total preoccupation—and nothing and no one outside the theatre on the lake had had any significance.

But now Bram must really be recovering. Both times before when she had called, she had been stonewalled by a butler's voice saying that Mr Calthrop was too indisposed to come to the telephone even though, she had no doubt, there was an extension beside his bed. So she had left her number and not pressed her point.

But if Bram had now called her, it *must* mean that he was well enough to make his own decision about who he would or would not speak to.

She had gone straight to the telephone but now she paused and looked at it and Cindy's note. What was she going to say? And—far more significantly—what did Bram want to say to her?

She almost grabbed the telephone and dialled the long distance operator's number.

'Calthrop residence!' The same stonewall butler's voice came down the line when the operator finally connected them.

'Mr Calthrop, please!' Carly sucked her cheeks to get more moisture into her mouth. 'Mr *Brampton* Calthrop!' Although there was no other Mr Calthrop in the house; just Bram's mother and a divorced sister. Carly had never met them; they were part of Bram's other life, quite separate from the theatre and big business.

'May I tell Mr Calthrop who is calling?'

It must be Jeeves or Aubrey Smith come back to life from wherever expatriate English actors went when they died after a lifetime of playing stiff upper lip British types in Hollywood. The man was just too English and too butler-ish to be true! Carly stifled a giggle of sheer nervousness.

'Miss Mason! Carly Mason. I'm returning Mr Calthrop's call!'

'Just a moment, madam!'

It was a long moment and when the phone was again picked up, it was still the butler's voice, not Bram's. 'I'm sorry, madam, but Mr Calthrop is indisposed!'

'But he called me! He wants me to speak to him!'

'I'm sorry, madam!' The butler was not going to be swayed. 'Do you wish to leave a message for Mr Calthrop?'

'No, no message! Thank you! Goodbye!' Carly put down the telephone. She could leave all the messages she liked but they would never get to Bram.

It might have taken a near fatal accident to do it but the Calthrop family—*mère et fille*—had got their straying son and brother back again. They had reclaimed him from the jaws of death—or, and this was probably much worse, they had snatched him from the clutches of a designing actress—and they had absolutely no intention of allowing him to fall under her influence again. ·

CHAPTER FOUR

To anyone more than a foot away, the tiny tightening of facial muscles and the sharp, exasperated hiss of breath would have been indiscernible but Nina and Trigorin were alone, acting out their scene on a bare stage which, one day soon, would be transformed by the alchemy of carpenters and set designers into Daniel's vision of a nineteenth century Russian country house.

The scene had been going well but a movement in the wings, just on the edge of her line of vision, had affected Carly's concentration. She was off a beat as she responded to one of Ed McMaster's lines and the older actor's face told her that he knew it and was not pleased.

'I'm sorry, Ed!' There wasn't time to say it, any more than there was time to do anything these days except eat, sleep and dream the parts that she was playing. Nina, Trelawney, the second lead in a new play Daniel had specially commissioned and then, thankfully, only a very small part in the fourth and last production of the season.

It was hard. Harder than anything she had ever done before; perhaps because of the man hidden in the darkness of the auditorium, unseen but with a sense of his presence always there, watching, assessing, hearing her every word and move.

Again—and again and again and again—whether onstage in rehearsal or alone, studying, in her narrow room, she drove herself to reach a standard of excellence she often despaired of achieving. Never before had she driven herself so ruthlessly that she lost weight and never had work been so much the subject of so many restless dreams.

Robin had once more stayed in the narrow house the previous night but, long before he had slipped quietly out of Cindy's room, Carly had been awake, going through moves, repeating lines, thinking—always thinking—what she could do to achieve her goal of making Nina not just young and charming, but full of the haunting incandescence on which the whole play stood or fell.

With Bram, it had been easy. The knowledge that Bram had been always out there, in the darkness of the theatre in San Francisco, had given her a sense of security. She was good, she knew she was, and Bram was giving her the chance to prove it.

Here, though, a pair of far more critical eyes were always somewhere out there in the darkness watching her—in the light of the early morning, Carly had turned restlessly in her narrow bed—not blinded by infatuation but dispassionately appraising and totally professional.

'Good!' The scene ended; there was a beat and Daniel's voice came from the auditorium. 'It's come along a lot since yesterday!' Carly heard three seats slap back as he got up, quickly followed by his assistant and secretary. 'No notes! I'll see you both in the morning!'

'Not me, thank God!' Even for an actor as experienced as Ed McMaster, the strain was showing. 'I'm not called until tomorrow afternoon!'

'In that case,' Daniel's slightly roughened voice had a wry edge, 'I wish you a pleasant night and an undisturbed morning's sleep. Think of the working population when you do surface!'

'I'll do that!' Ed was already turning towards the wings. ''Night, Daniel!'

'Goodnight, Ed!' There was a pause. 'Charlotte!' Carly could hear, if she could not see, the already half turned back.

'Goodnight!' She made her goodnights in a rush and left the stage. Ed had gone and she had been dismissed. But—what had she been waiting for? A pat on the back? Daniel telling her that she was marvellous?

She collected her tote bag from the stage manager's cubby hole in the wings, said a few more goodnights and went outside. Even this late in the spring, it was almost dark. She could smell, but not see, the lilac trees planted around the little outside cafeteria area which adjoined the theatre's larger and much more formal indoor restaurant.

Theatre on the Lake was a total concept, along the lines of Nottingham and Chichester in England. So far from the nearest large population centre—in this case, Toronto—it could not survive, even with subsidies, unless it offered more than just a play. The audience had to have reason to come for a whole day so that they would eat in the cafeteria or restaurant, stroll through the parkland beside the lake and maybe buy souvenirs from the two gift shops in the big foyer which offered attractively packaged and presented items of theatrical memorabilia.

For the more serious theatregoers, workshops were even planned, to be run by Daniel's assistant.

Carly had noticed she was down for four. They were to be rap sessions, Harley had explained; free interchange between cast members and audience and potential audience. There was certainly going to be coffee and doughnuts—also free—and, if there was a demand, Harley had ideas about cast members and audience getting together and acting out a few impromptu scenes.

The days of 'us' and 'them' were gone, Harley had explained over the chorus of general groans, the general public had to be involved. Rather than complain, Harley had said rather waspishly, they ought to consider themselves lucky to be here, anyway, and view the workshops as no more than a way of paying their dues by trying to ensure that the theatre was still there for the generations of unborn actors coming after them.

But for all Harley's philosophical philanthropy, Carly was still dreading it. The thought of improvising—acting not just with amateurs but with people who were totally unknown to her—

was terrifying. She was sure she would seize up, go dumb and look a fool. Much worse than first night nerves, she felt shivery and queasy whenever she thought of it. The only two things on her side were, first, that the workshops were not scheduled to begin until well after the season had got into its stride and the second, that Daniel had nothing to do with them.

The one thing in all the preparation for the season—frontstage, backstage, everything from financial backing and maintaining good relations with the people in the town to the casting of the last non-speaking drama student for the last non-speaking part—in which Daniel, as overall director, had no part.

Daniel! Carly speeded up on her way back to the narrow house. In the past ten years, she had been so careful not to think of him and now circumstance had made him a factor in her every waking thought.

She heard the music well before she got there; an up-beat reggae tune floating through the open windows and the sound of laughter and far too many voices coming down what should have been a quiet Main Street.

'Oh, no!' She groaned and a couple of residents out on their evening stroll turned and looked at her.

An actress! Who else could it be in those extraordinary clothes. Even with the business it would bring, it still wasn't worth having a theatre in their quiet town if it meant all this noise and nuisance.

Carly couldn't hear but she could guess the conversation that started up immediately the couple turned the corner. Young women walking the streets in leg warmers and tights were bad enough—now they had orgies to contend with.

Carly guessed and sympathised. She wanted home, bed and sleep, in that order; what she was going to get was a wild party and hours of noise.

Someone in the company—Carly was past remembering who—had a birthday and Angela had offered their house for the celebrations. And they were celebrations that were getting somewhat out of hand judging by the number of giggling, recumbent figures around which she had to pick her way when she went in through the front gate and walked across the lawn to the verandah.

'Keep it down, will you?' Somewhere inside the house, Robin, at least, was trying to restore some sort of order. 'We've got to live with the people in this town for the whole summer! We want them on our side, remember? Not getting up petitions to close the theatre down!'

Carly heard him as she manoeuvred her way between two youths propping up the open doorway. They were bikers; gate-crashers from out of town, drawn by the jungle drums that always seemed to announce a party and dressed in leather and bare chests with enough chains to stock a whole stageful of Jacob Marley's ghosts.

As Robin finished, one of them raised the hand not holding a can of beer and waved a limp wrist in the general direction of Robin's pink satin shirt. They both sniggered.

'Carly! Hi! Carly!' A slightly tipsy Angela pushed her way up to her. 'Isn't this fun?' Totally oblivious of the potential menace posed by the two bikers, she gazed around at the roomful of sweating faces and bodies gyrating frantically to the beat of stereo music with the expression of a hostess who considers her job well done. 'Mike says he's never had such a birthday!' she added complacently.

'No, I don't suppose he has!' Carly said drily. In part she could understand. They had all been driven hard—forgetting that she had left him at the theatre, she instinctively looked around for Daniel—and this was no more than a release of tension. But—

'Here! Have a drink!' Carly had caught sight of Robin, harassed looking in spite of the flamboyant pink of his satin shirt but, before she could do anything about getting to him and lending him her support, Angela was thrusting a glass underneath her nose. 'It's wine——' Angela tried to focus on the wildly slopping contents but gave up with a giggle, '—I think!'

'No, I don't——!'

'Oh, come on, Carly, don't be such a wet! A little drink won't hurt you and you're miles behind the rest of us! Unless,' blurry blue eyes narrowed suddenly and Angela turned truculent, 'unless it's drinking out of my glass that bothers you!'

'No, of course not!' Carly changed what she

had been going to say and took the warm, wet, sticky glass. There was going to be a scene if she wasn't careful. Things had never quite got back to being what they were since the evening when Angela had been on the receiving end of her tongue. Angela thought she was a snob, that much was obvious and if Angela was having second thoughts about them sharing, she, herself, was more and more questioning the wisdom of being in a house in which there never seemed to be just the three of them. If it wasn't Robin, it was two or three of the others lazing around on the verandah or joining them for meals and now—this party. She looked around the wildly gyrating room.

She couldn't remember the last time she had come home to total peace and quiet and the hotel on the green was beginning to look more and more appealing. Not that she could ever move there—she could just imagine the bad blood if she did.

As far as the company was concerned, it would be separate camps again, just like San Francisco. Most of them on Angela and Cindy's side as the news got round and the rest struggling to stay neutral, leaving her once more as the outsider.

Untouched glass in hand, she tried to push her way unobtrusively towards the stairway and escape up to her room. No, she decided, ideas about moving out and into the hotel were just about as far fetched as the idea of moving in with Daniel.

'Oh!' She came back to earth to find someone bumping into her and Angela's drink spilling all over her. 'I'm sorry!' No one was listening. 'Excuse me! I have to go upstairs and change!'

On the stereo, Peter Tosh and his Rastafarians pounded on. One-beat; two-beat; three-beat; four! The music rose through two ceilings and a floor and made the glass rattle on the night table in Carly's attic room. She had given up trying to keep track of time; given up even attempting to learn more lines and was just lying there, on the bed, willing it all to end.

Above the din of music and high-pitched laughter, she heard a car draw up outside and a door slammed. If car doors could slam authoritatively, this one had authority. *Police!* Carly supposed it was inevitable. What Robin had been so concerned about was happening. Trouble with the town. It must be close to midnight—if not later—and someone, patience stretched beyond endurance by mindless noise and complete lack of consideration, had finally picked up his or her telephone and complained.

The music stopped suddenly and the silence was deafening. Carly listened. This cop had class, she acknowledged admiringly. Forty, fifty, sixty people—she had no idea how many might have been milling around downstairs—had turned from a noisy, screeching mob into a well disciplined Sunday School class.

She could still hear voices, but they were quiet and subdued. She also heard the sound of breaking glass, followed by a quick apology but otherwise, all she heard were footsteps going towards the gate and then off along the sidewalk and the muted roar of motor bikes and the cars being driven quietly away.

Peace descended; then two sets of footsteps came upstairs and turned off on the first landing. Cindy and Angela. Robin was still talking though. She could hear him through her partly open window, carrying on a quiet conversation in the garden with a much deeper voice, and then he said goodnight. Robin obviously did not plan to stay on this particular night.

Carly stretched and got up off the bed and started to undress. It must look like a disaster zone downstairs, but she wouldn't think of that. At least, not until the morning when, although she had played no part in organising the party, conscience or expectation would doubtless oblige her to do her share of clearing up.

She heard more footsteps on the stairs. Things, then, hadn't really changed that much. After going a little way down the street, Robin had obviously turned around and doubled back. But these footsteps didn't stop at Cindy's room. They came on up and stopped outside her door. Puzzled, but still not really alarmed, Carly pulled on her cotton robe over nothing underneath and went towards it. Someone knocked.

'Who is it?'

'Daniel!'

Her heart did wild things in her chest and the hand half way to the door stopped motionless in mid-air.

'May I come in!'

'Of course!' Somehow she not only found her voice but it sounded natural. 'The door's not locked!'

She fell back into the angle between the night table and her bed as the white-painted door began to open. The only way to play this particular scene was as if nothing untoward was happening. So! It was Daniel who was coming in! How many other times had Daniel been in her room at this time of night. Hundreds when they were married—the only problem was that it had been thousands of nights since then.

'Charlotte!' He came in and closed the door and acknowledged her with a slight nod as he stood there, back against the jamb, arms folded and eyes steady above the crooked question mark of his characteristic little smile. 'I'm sorry if I woke you up!'

'You didn't!' One hand went automatically to her exposed throat and the other sketched a fluttery little gesture in the direction of the night table and her open script. 'I was working,' she explained. 'Learning lines!' It was a relief to have an excuse to look away. Where they rested on her face and neck, his eyes were burning her.

'I'm surprised you could concentrate on anything with that racket going on!'

Two things slipped suddenly into place. Firstly, that he was holding her responsible for the party—she was older than Cindy and Angela; should have more commonsense—and secondly that it had been Daniel who had brought the festivities so sharply to an end.

'It was you, then!'

'Me?' When she glanced back, his look was mildly curious.

'Downstairs! Earlier! Getting everyone to go home!' In front of an audience, it was easy but in front of him, she could not control her breath. The words came out in a disconnected, jerky rush. Someone—Robin, probably—had called him and bikers, gatecrashers and celebrating members of the company had taken one look and quietly disappeared. Who needed police when they could have Daniel Stone? She stole a glance at the special brand of powerful stillness leaning up against her door. 'And you're blaming me, I suppose?' she went on defensively. His eyebrows rose. 'For the party; for the noise?'

'Why should I when I gather you had nothing to do with it?' He shifted slightly. 'Those responsible already know how I feel and, as far as I'm concerned, the incident is now closed!' Except that there would be no more parties getting out of hand and the town's residents would sleep undisturbed in their beds.

Thank you, Robin! Thank you for telling him it wasn't me! Carly saw the expression on Daniel's face and made a mental note to consider herself in Robin Thurgood's debt.

'But then——?' Now she was really nervous. If it wasn't to hand out blame, what was Daniel doing here? 'Then,' she said, 'what do you want?'

'To talk!' In the combination light of street

lamp coming through the window and the pinkish glow from the lamp on her bedside table, his eyes were luminous in their frame of thick, black lashes.

'To talk? What about?' It came out in a much more hostile fashion than she intended and she saw Daniel's lips tighten and the light in his eyes go out.

'Your work,' he said.

'Oh!' What else would Daniel want to talk to her about? 'I would have thought you could have done that in the theatre!' she said, deflated.

'I could have,' he confirmed, 'except that what I have to say doesn't need an audience and whenever I keep anyone back, gossip has a habit of starting up!'

And she could imagine the sort of gossip he had in mind. The company had been together for perhaps six weeks but the routine pairings were already taking place—Robin and Cindy were a case in point—and the petty rivalries and jealousies. Daniel Stone and Carly—Charlotte—Mason! And why not? Not only was Daniel unattached but, when her predecessor had suddenly dropped out, Daniel had taken off, leaving the company to his assistant's tender mercies, only to return with a brief, unexplained announcement that he had hired an actress no one had ever heard of to take Margaret Duboisson's place.

It was all too close to home. A little digging by someone a little more curious—or malicious—than the rest, could easily uncover the unknown fact that Carly—Charlotte—Mason had once been Daniel Stone's wife.

'Yes,' she said, 'I see. But I hardly think coming up here, now——' she meant the room and time, 'is going to do either of our reputations any good!'

'Do you really think anyone is going to mention it?' He meant Cindy and Angela downstairs.

She looked away from him. 'No,' she muttered. 'No, I don't!'

Cindy and Angela—even if they had heard him come upstairs—would be only too pleased to close their eyes and ears. After tonight's party and what Daniel had no doubt had to say, Cindy and Angela would be only too pleased to keep their jobs.

'It seems, then, that we agree at last!' He smiled and straightened from the door, costing her a few inches of her precious space. In the narrow room, he was now so close that she could see the fine grain of his skin and feel the turbulence his voice caused in the air.

'Then what did you want to say?' she asked him jerkily. 'About my work, I mean! You're not satisfied?'

'On the contrary, I'm very satisfied!' Head on one side, he studied her with his little glinting smile. 'As far as it goes!'

'And what exactly is that supposed to mean?' She could feel her skin warming under the scrutiny of his eyes.

'That you're trying too hard!' he stated flatly. 'What happened with Ed today, for instance!'

No one could have seen, no one could possibly have seen—especially someone sitting twenty or so rows back in a darkened auditorium—how angry Ed McMaster had been earlier when a movement in the wings had spoiled her concentration and caused her, in her turn, to spoil the delivery of one of his best lines. It had shaken her—that 'if looks could kill' look—and it had taken her a long time to recover, but surely she should have been professional enough to hide what she was feeling and no one should have seen. But Daniel had—and Daniel had seized this unexpected opportunity to come and tell her so.

'I'm sorry!' She deliberately misunderstood. 'I didn't realise that, in order to get your unqualified approval, I'm expected to let another actor walk all over me!'

'Will you stop that!' The face was hard but the voice was weary. 'I thought you might have changed but . . .' For once, Daniel left a sentence hanging in the air. 'Ambition!' He was almost talking to himself. 'Haven't you realised yet what a destructive force that is?'

'Whereas you've no longer any need to be ambitious! You've got there, haven't you? To the very top! Daniel Stone! Internationally known director!' What was making her behave like this? She couldn't stop—some inner force was driving her. Something way beyond her ability to control.

'Yes!' The temperature dropped to zero with his voice. 'I've got there and so will you, if you give yourself a chance. Relax, don't try so hard!'

He took a step towards her and she instinctively stepped back; stopped by the hard edge of the night table pressing against her legs. 'Oh, don't worry!' His sneer cut through her to the bone. 'I told you! I'm here to talk about your work! Anything else is irrelevant!' Like her cotton robe wrapping itself around her legs and making it obvious she wore nothing underneath.

Carly began to tremble but not with fear. She hated Daniel Stone. For a moment, he had made her remember how it was. Their bodies fitting, moving, and all the world she wanted reflected in his eyes. But that had been so long ago and now a stranger with a hard, clipped voice, was talking as if they had only just that moment met.

'And my work is not irrelevant?' She bit it out, pleased this time with her control.

'No, it's not!' He matched her, ice for ice. This was Daniel? She found it difficult to believe. Underneath the prematurely greying hair was the man she had once loved. The man who, in another place—another time—would have taken her in his arms, regardless of her mood, and let his lips slide down to the shadow between her breasts. Her whole body stirred. Yes! This was Daniel.

'*You*,' it took a second for what he was saying to make sense, 'are the lynchpin on which this first production rests. The crux, the fulcrum— whichever word you care to use. I chose you because I thought you had the strength to make this production soar. Nina! *The Seagull!* Remember, Charlotte?' Like one of the seagulls they had watched on their honeymoon, diving down on the surface of the waves, he was attacking her. 'People depend on you! The whole future of this season,' he stopped and judged not her, in the outline of her clinging robe, but the words in the forefront of his mind, 'the careers of everyone concerned,' he was satisfied and the words flowed smoothly on, 'depend on your ability to make the audience believe!'

'And you don't think I have that ability?' It was hard to say. With Bram there had never been that doubt; there had always been the Calthrop millions. If she failed, it would be no more than a blow to her self esteem. Bram would pay. He would pick up the tab and the people with whom she had been working could go on to other things. But here, it was different. Grants, political manoeuvrings, everything had gone into the creation of this theatre on the lake. And Daniel cared. His intensity, his sheer force, could leave her in no doubt of that.

'No! Not doubtful!' Daniel picked up her words. 'Absolutely convinced!' His hand on her wrist sent sparks flying up her arm.

'Then fire me!' It was ridiculous. No director could fire his leading lady so close to opening night.

'I would!' Typically Daniel, he proved her wrong. Even with his face so close to hers, she could see nothing to show he had the slightest hesitation in what he said. 'I would! Believe me, Charlote, I really would!'

'Then?' For a moment she relaxed.

'Except that I have no choice!' His eyes bored into her. 'Once I followed an intuition—a gut hunch—that sent me to San Francisco to find an actress who had once been my wife!' Was it her imagination, or had he really wavered when he had come to that last word? The fingers on Carly's wrist clamped tight and drove all other thinking from her mind. 'But I don't have that choice again,' he said. 'You're here! I stand or fall on what you do. Just like the rest,' lips inches from her own twisted in a wry smile, 'you make or break my being here!'

One moment, he was looking down at her and the next there was deep black. Daniel was kissing her; his mouth hard against her parted lips and his free hand sliding along her back. She felt him, every inch of him, as he pulled her to him in a long caress. Breasts melted and then thighs as she remembered. *This* was Daniel. This long strength of body against which she arched her back.

Daniel! Could she ever imagine herself in love with anyone except this man?

He held her from him as she reached the thought and she saw the expression on his face. Daniel! Daniel Stone! The director who would do anything to make his point.

'That's right, Charlotte!' Above her, eyes gazing down and mocking through narrowed lids told her everything she had to know. 'That's exactly what I'm telling you!' he drawled. 'Relax like that and none of us will have anything to be worried about from the critics on opening night!'

'Is that all?' She had never been so humiliated in her life.

'Yes!' He studied her. 'That's all!'

'Then perhaps if you'd be kind enough to let me go—and leave!' She looked pointedly down at the fingers still on her shoulders and then towards the door. 'Perhaps I can get some sleep! I assume this out of hours rehearsal session doesn't mean I can be late in in the morning!'

His hands dropped from her shoulders, leaving just the memory of their pressure burning through her robe. 'No,' he said, 'it doesn't! I'll expect you there at nine. Goodnight, Charlotte!'

She deliberately turned away and, a second later, she heard the door close.

The house was quiet after the front gate clicked shut and the sound of Daniel's car disappeared along the street but Carly went on standing exactly where she was.

Ten years ago, she had made a resolution; never, ever to look back with regret on the ending of her marriage. She had refused to waste her life dwelling on the might-have-been but now all the feeling that had been repressed but not resolved had been brought boiling to the surface of her mind.

Why? *Why* had Daniel done this to her? But even as she asked herself the question, she knew the answer. He had done it for the play—his precious play and, having achieved his purpose, he had left.

To him, his kiss had been nothing more than a means of showing her that she was capable of giving the emotion he wanted to see projected when she was on stage. He didn't care how many memories he had awakened or what he had done to her peace of mind.

Perhaps if there had been someone else between now and Daniel, it would have been easier but affairs had always set her teeth on edge and stopped her short of them. Bram had come the closest—Carly gave a rueful little smile—but even Bram had not had his affair.

But this was pointless! Slipping off her robe, Carly got quickly into bed and felt the coolness of the sheets against the full length of her body. Another legacy from Daniel.

All properly brought up girls wore nightdresses but—'Why bother to put it on when I only have to take it off again?' A smiling Daniel had asked the question on the first night of their honeymoon, the one and only time he had ever had to slide a nightdress off above her head.

Carly shifted restlessly. What was she so concerned about? Some things never died, that's all, and the memory of loving Daniel was obviously one of them. It was like riding a bicycle—God! What on earth had put that comparison into her head? But it was the same. Once you had learned the knack, it never left you but that didn't mean you ever had to ride a bicycle again.

She hunched the single sheet around her shoulders and turned over to face the wall. So! She had once been hopelessly in love with Daniel and perhaps part of her still was but that didn't mean she would ever go back to him.

'Carly!' The soft voice and the persistence of the even softer knocking on her door brought her out of a heavy, unrefreshing sleep. She put out a hand and groped for her watch on the night table beside her bed. Eight-thirty! Her eyes focused on the tiny hands and she was immediately awake. Rehearsals started at nine o'clock.

'Who is it?' She was out of bed and pulling on her robe before she called.

'It's Cindy!' The door opened a crack. 'Can I come in?'

'Yes, of course!' Carly answered automatically. She had thirty minutes to shower and dress and get herself onstage.

'I didn't know if I should come up or not?' A hand holding a glass of orange juice appeared around the door, followed by Cindy's apologetic face.

'Why shouldn't you come up?' Carly shot her a suspicious glance. Had Cindy's first look been towards the bed?

Daniel had probably been right when he had said that neither Cindy nor Angela would either choose or want to know who had come up to her room last night but Daniel's distinctive voice would carry easily and it would have only had to float down about eight feet to be heard in Cindy and Angela's rooms.

Was that what Cindy had been looking for? Any trace that Daniel had spent the night?

'I meant, when we didn't hear you getting up, we didn't know whether we should come and wake you up or not! I mean,' Cindy carefully put the full glass down, avoiding Carly's face, 'you're probably still pretty mad about last night!'

Carly let out her breath and smiled. The orange juice was a peace offering and she was being paranoid. Cindy was talking about the party and, although she doubtless had Daniel on her mind, it was not in that particular way.

'Not that you've not got every right to be!' Cindy went on in a rush of double negatives. 'Angela's terrified. She's thinking of just packing up and going home!'

'I didn't realise I was so frightening!' Carly tried to get round her to the door. 'Look, Cindy, I must get . . .!'

'No! Not of you!' They had probably drawn lots, Carly imagined. Cindy and Angela. Loser to come upstairs and test the temperature of the atmosphere. 'We're neither of us frightened of you!' Cindy gave a shaky smile. 'It's Mr Stone. I mean, I know we should never have had the party—at least, the party was all right, it was the way it got out of hand. I know we said everybody—but we'd no idea all those people would turn up—and then Mr Stone said . . .!' Cindy's voice trailed away and she looked at Carly with huge, tragic eyes, '. . . well, it wasn't what he said exactly, it was . . .!' She trailed away again. 'Do you know?' she seemed incredulous. 'He never raised his voice! Not once! But Angela's terrified! I don't think she slept all night!'

Oh, yes, she knew! Daniel had never raised his

voice with her. Not when he was really angry; deep down, stone cold, grimly angry.

'Anyway, when we didn't hear you getting up——' Just as neither of them *had* probably registered Daniel coming to her room last night. When you had just been on the end of a lashing from Daniel's tongue, the world could end without you noticing. '—We thought perhaps—well, Angela did—well,' brown eyes swivelled away and swivelled back, 'we both did really . . .!'

Get on with it, Cindy. Say what you want to say and then let me get dressed. Conscious of every second passing, it was an effort to hold back the words.

'What did you both think?' Sometimes her ability as an actress quite amazed her. Inside, she was seething with impatience and yet her voice was not just encouraging, it was calm.

Cindy smiled at her gratefully. 'We thought, perhaps, you could speak to Mr Stone. Tell him that we're really sorry and that nothing like it will ever happen again!' she blurted out.

'But surely you've already told him that yourselves?' Suddenly, she felt so old. She had been younger than Cindy when she had first met Daniel and now, she was what? Eight years older? Exactly the length of time since she had last seen Daniel.

A hearing for discovery, they had called it. A hearing to discover the facts behind the breakdown of their marriage. A short, formal, question and answer session in a windowless court office with only their solicitors and a court stenographer present. It had ended with Daniel going stiff-backed through the door.

'Oh, yes, we have!' Cindy hastened to assure her.

It had been eight years between that awful day and Daniel's totally unexpected reappearance in her life.

'But we thought, perhaps, that if you told him again for us it might mean more coming from you! Please, Carly!' Huge brown eyes once more pleaded. 'Please!'

'Oh, all right! I'll see what I can do!' Anything to get Cindy out of her room and get started with her day. She now, she saw, had twenty minutes.

'Thank you, Carly! We'll never forget it! Really we won't!' Cindy's gratitude took another two.

It wasn't until she was on her way to the theatre, damp hair flying and drying as she ran along, that it occurred to her to wonder just why Cindy and Angela should think that she had any influence with Daniel Stone.

CHAPTER FIVE

INCREDIBLY, the day went well. Perhaps it was because she was so preoccupied but, for the first time since rehearsals started, Carly found herself relaxing and forgetting the mechanics of the moves and words and letting Nina's personality take her over.

'I can see we're going to have to watch ourselves if we don't want you stealing *all* the notices on opening night!'

'I hardly think that's likely!' Carly glanced at the speaker in the mirror.

Polly Marshall was in her middle thirties. Just as she was chronologically much older than her own character, Nina, so Polly was about twelve years too young for her part of Trigorin's long-time mistress, Madame Arkadin.

But Carly could understand why Daniel had chosen her. Polly had a shrewdness, an air of worldly wisdom in her almond eyes that, combined with a certain voluptuousness of figure, gave the impression that she had seen, done and sampled everything. It was hard to imagine that Polly Marshall had ever really been young.

'Mmm!' Polly looked at her sidelong in the mirror. 'Maybe! Maybe not!'

They were sharing a dressing room; not that it

was yet a dressing room in the full sense of the word. There were no costumes on the racks, no powder or sticks and jars of make-up on the long, formica topped dressing table counter. And the room was new; it did not yet have that indefinable smell of size and paint and powder which was— Carly's stomach swooped—theatre.

On the night, the naked light bulbs on all four sides of the mirror would be switched on, exposing every line and flaw and wrinkle but, for now, the room was lit by just one overhead strip of lighting and the counter beneath the mirror held nothing more exotic than two boxes of paper tissues, their purses and a scatter of small belongings.

'You're too modest!' Polly seemed totally absorbed in blotting lipstick with a paper tissue. 'Incidentally,' it was just too casual as she finished and Carly tensed, 'what had you been doing before Daniel found you? You're so good——' throw in a compliment to take the edge off a too blatant curiosity, '—and yet none of us had ever heard of you before!'

'Oh, you know!' Carly tried to shrug it off. 'I'd been working in the States and England. Plays, commercials, television—the usual sort of thing!'

'Really?' There was another sidelong glance. 'And when did you meet Daniel?'

'In England, years ago!' Carly began to brush her hair with a fierce concentration. 'He was doing an audition!'

'And did you get the part?' Through the veil of hair, Polly's face was indistinct but not her voice.

No! We got married two weeks later. 'No!' she said.

'But Daniel remembered you?'

'Yes,' Carly put her brush down, 'I guess he did! Excuse me!' She got up, opened her canvas tote and shovelled in her purse and script; not *The Seagull*, those lines were already a part of her, but *Trelawney of the Wells*. 'I want to catch him before he leaves!'

That had not been well done! No revelations, that had been one of her conditions—or had it been one of Daniel's?—when she had agreed to come up here for the season. She stood or fell on her own talent, not on the fact that she had once been Mrs Daniel Stone and, although she had not let slip about their marriage, she had certainly just said too much—or had it been too little? Anyway, the net result was that Polly's antennae, finely tuned for gossip, were already clearly waving.

And on top of everything, she had had to use the truth to get herself out of the room. Why on earth had she had to say that she wanted to see Daniel. She could have been going home—everyone else was—she could have been going anywhere. But she had had to say that she was going to see Daniel and why—she could almost hear the workings of Polly Marshall's mind—why would Charlotte Mason be in such a rush to have a private word with Daniel Stone?

Carly stopped outside the door of Daniel's office further along the narrow backstage corridor, hitched her tote bag over her shoulder and pulled the strings tight. Perhaps Daniel wasn't there. She almost hoped he wasn't; at least, she could then tell Cindy that she'd tried.

She hadn't seen much of Cindy or Angela all day but whenever she had caught sight of them backstage, they had both been following her with big, imploring eyes. She had promised and she supposed she would have to go through with it but, knowing Daniel, he had probably not given the party a second thought. Once something had been settled to his satisfaction, that was it.

Right! Bracing herself, she raised her hand and knocked. In doing so, she caught sight of her watch. It really was late. Another long, hard gruelling day. She hardly knew why she had even bothered; Daniel would not be there.

'Come!' He looked preoccupied when she went in; and tired. Carly felt a flicker of sympathy and fought it down. 'Charlotte?' It seemed to take him a second to realise. 'What are you doing here?'

'I've come to apologise,' she said abruptly.

'Really?' Two dark eyebrows rose like wings above the question mark of his smile. 'I didn't think apologies were much in your line!'

'They're not!' She could deal with him like this. This was Daniel; mocking, cynical, slightly amused. 'It's Cindy and Angela I'm apologising for, not me! They want me to make their peace with you!'

He looked genuinely bemused. 'Cindy and Angela?'

'The girls I room with!' she explained.

'Ah, yes!' Now he remembered. 'Our young party givers! And what are they apologising for?'

'For being stupid—silly—all the things you doubtless told them they were last night!' Carly paused; making peace for someone else was difficult. 'They're also frightened you might be going to let them go!'

'Fire them?' Daniel frowned. 'Why should I do that? I'm sure they got my point last night!'

'Yes,' she said, 'I'm sure they did!'

She stood there awkwardly; no tights and leg warmers tonight but a white, Madras cotton dress held in at the waist with a broad, red satin belt and her hair falling softly against her shoulders.

'And now . . .!'

And now would she please leave and let him get on with his work. It was all there in the weary stretch of the long body and the look away from her to the paper covered desk and then the door.

'. . . and now, what would you say about coming for a drink?'

'What?' She was stunned.

'It's been a long day!' He got up, towering over her, and ran a hand through his thick mass of grey flecked hair. 'Did you hear that one of our financial backers has dropped out?'

'Yes!' It had been common knowledge from the moment she got in. The theatre was part government subsidised and part privately financed and now a large part of the privately invested money had been withdrawn. Someone had died or someone had decided they wanted a larger return on their investment—backstage rumour had varied on this point—but the result was that, from being financially secure, not just the theatre but this first season was now in jeopardy and someone—Daniel—had to find the means of making up the shortfall.

She noticed now that the telephone on his desk had been pulled into the centre and was surrounded by torn off sheets of scratch pad, covered with figures and random scribblings. Daniel had obviously been calling Toronto or New York; any of the big money markets where he might find new backers to the tune of, perhaps, a million dollars. It was another burden added to the many—one which had taken him away from most of the day's rehearsals and left them in the hands of his assistant—and it was obviously why he was still here.

'Now,' he got his jacket from the back of his chair and slung it across one shoulder, 'what about that drink?'

'All right!' If he could pretend last night had never happened, then so could she. 'Just *one* drink would be nice,' she emphasised. 'But where?'

'Where indeed?' His eyes ran over her, lambent and privately amused. 'The hotel perhaps?'

'Won't that be a little public?' The King Edward Hotel in town had developed into an informal green room for some of the older members of the company.

Her own verandah where the beer, if not quite free, could at least be drunk at take-out prices, might have become the gathering place for the younger ones—the less senior ones—but for people like Ed McMaster and Polly Marshall, it was the lounge bar of the King Edward. If Daniel wanted the world to know that Charlotte Mason was the subject of some special interest, all he had to do was to walk her into that hotel.

'In that case,' his hand was somehow underneath her elbow and was guiding her through his office door, 'we'll have to think of somewhere else!'

His open sports car was the only one left in the theatre car park and, getting into it, Carly immediately went back ten years. It had been a sports car then.

'You can't possibly go in an open car, to say nothing of the fact that Daniel certainly shouldn't be driving you! It's unlucky for the groom to see the bride before the ceremony—and what about your hair?'

Her hair, with its scattering of tiny rosebuds, could fly to the four corners of the earth for all she cared and, as for luck, who needed luck when they were so much in love. Carly had heard her mother rattling on but all she was listening for was the door. In a minute, it would open and Daniel would be there. She had smoothed a dress very much like the one she was now wearing, except that this was cotton and that had been made of silk. In a minute, that door would open and she would see the man with whom she was going to spend her life.

Carly sighed. Oh to be eighteen again and so blithely confident.

The dark blue sports car—descendant of the red one that had taken her to her wedding—turned out of the theatre car park and Daniel paused at the end of the laneway leading on to Main Street before turning left again and driving at a steady speed away from the town centre and the King Edward.

'Where are we going?' She shot it at him suspiciously as store fronts and houses disappeared behind them and they headed towards the open country.

In the gathering twilight, white teeth glinted. 'Home!' he said.

Her stomach did a violent somersault. 'Your house?'

'Why not?' This time she got a look and the rush of wind made his mouth curl at the corners. 'It's there, it's empty and I'm tired and I need a shower!'

'Oh!' She settled back into her seat. Where else had she expected him to take her? It was logical and logic had always been one of Daniel's strong points. Logical about his reasons for not pushing her career; logical, even, about the ending of their marriage once, that was, he had made up his mind.

Besides, she was being foolish. It was sheer chance she was here, anyway. Daniel was tired and Daniel needed company and she had just happened to walk into his office at the right time. It could just as well have been Polly Marshall sitting with the force of gravity pressing her back against the leather seat as the trees whipped past and the speedometer needle wavered close to triple figures.

They turned again, this time more quickly and this time into a narrow, private drive. Thrown against him, Carly felt his arm against her shoulder. She could smell him. Competing with the almost overpowering scent of the blossom trees that lined the drive was the hard, nutty fragrance she would always associate with Daniel. Whenever he had had to leave her for an early rehearsal call, she had always moved across the suddenly empty bed, fitting her body into the warmth his had left and burying her face into his pillow. Smell was not a sense normally associated with romance but, lying there, eyes closed, head half hidden, she could spin out the moment and make believe she was still in Daniel's arms.

'Wake up! We've arrived!' Another time, another place and she was sitting watching Daniel walk around in front of the Morgan to come and open her door.

'Thank you!' Getting out, Carly saw a house with a long façade gleaming whitely in the gathering darkness. Trees rustled overhead, a nightbird called and lights shone through two downstairs windows.

As they walked up the shallow flight of steps leading to the front door, Daniel remarked on them. 'Eva must still be here!' he said comfortably.

'Eva?' She felt a moment's panic.

He bent his head above hers with a smile. Surely her reaction to another woman's name couldn't have been that obvious? 'My house-keeper,' he said laconically. 'She comes with the territory!'

'Oh, I see!' Carly felt uncomfortable.

'This place used to belong to old man Tyler,' Daniel explained, 'the property tycoon. He also owned the land where they built the theatre. It was all part and parcel of his will. A theatre for the town and a house for the artistic director.' His explanation took them through into a black and white tiled entrance hall with an impressive flight of stairs curving to an upper landing. There was darkness on one side of the hall; the lights were shining softly through a doorway on the other. 'Through here!' He stood back to let her precede him into a room that was half library and half lounge. 'It's a pity he didn't realise how much money it takes to run a theatre nowadays!' Daniel said ruefully. 'If he had, he might have left us another million then, perhaps, we wouldn't be in the financial trouble we're in now. Anyway ...!' His attention went to a sheet of paper propped up obviously on a small side table.

Carly stood there while he read it, uncomfortable with the memories that were being conjured up.

They hadn't had a house like this, of course. It had just been a garden flat but—behind Daniel's back, she gave a little shrug—how many times had Daniel come home just like this, full of his day, and she had stood there waiting until he was ready to give her just a little of his attention.

'It seems that we're to be alone, after all!' A

dark head, touched with light and turned to bronze was lifted in her direction and she had everything she had ever wanted of his attention. 'Eva's gone!' This time all her reaction was to the man. 'She's left some sort of salad in the fridge, apparently!' Daniel folded paper between long brown fingers and threw it casually in the basket beside the table. 'And there should be wine!'

'I'll get it!' Carly turned abruptly on her heel. 'Didn't you say you wanted to take a shower?'

She found the kitchen, the salad and the wine. She also found a record and put it on the stereo in the combination library and lounge.

'*Do you remember the kind of September when grass was green and corn was yellow?*' The crooner's voice came drifting across the room and Carly went instinctively to turn it off.

'Leave it!' This time it was Daniel's voice. 'It's a pleasant tune, as I remember!'

'Yes,' she choked, 'it is!'

They had had that record and played it endlessly.

'I've laid this table!' Anything—anything—to dispel this sudden flow of memories. 'But I haven't opened the wine!'

'Here! I'll do it!' Daniel came towards her. The shower had left his hair jet black and pale blue denim pants and shirt accentuated the darkness of his skin. They were alike, he had sometimes teased her. Both dark, both thoroughly un-English and both—she could still see the movement of his lips above hers as he had said it—far too much in love.

She found the corkscrew and held it out to him. She noticed she did it carefully so that, when he took it, their fingers wouldn't touch. She also noticed that she had a curious feeling of being outside herself; a little apart and above the woman sitting facing Daniel at the oval polished table in front of the french windows.

The table had a centrepiece of fruit. Rosy nectarines and grapes spilling over the sides of a silver bowl like some still life painting. Crystal and silver winked in the refulgent light but the table itself and the two people were in shadow, the woman with her head bent but the man watching her as she tried to eat.

They must have talked; indeed they did. The woman heard herself carrying on a conversation about safely impersonal things but inside, at a much deeper level, she was listening to her heart beat and feeling her skin tremble under the brush of deep grey eyes.

They should never have got married. They should never have succumbed to the fierce mutual wanting that had driven them to that dreary register office in Marylebone just two weeks after she had first looked up and seen Daniel walking towards her along a dusty backstage corridor.

Perhaps if the physical side of it had not been so perfect, she would not now be feeling so disturbed. But that particular magic had never died. She could storm off to bed after one of their blazing arguments and Daniel could follow—perhaps hours later—but he only had to touch

her, look at her in his special way, and she began
to melt.

'Would you like some coffee?'

'No! No, thank you!' His question was
innocuous enough, but suddenly her two selves
merged, leaving her unbearably self-conscious
and aware. 'Coffee keeps me awake if I have it too
late at night!'

'Really?' He smiled and Carly got abruptly to
her feet.

'I think I'll go outside,' she said breathlessly.
'It's hot in here!'

'Is it? I hadn't noticed!' Daniel followed her
with his private little smile. 'But here,' he got
quickly to his feet as she fumbled with the latch
on the french windows, 'let me do that!'

'No! It's all right! I can manage!' Mercifully,
the latch gave way before he reached her and she
went outside. The night was calm and beautiful
but its tranquillity failed to touch her. It must be
the wine. Too much wine, too little sleep: there
must be a million reasons why she was feeling as
she did; dry mouthed, aware, full of the feverish
tension of foreboding.

Daniel came up behind her and his breath
stirred the air against her hair.

'It's beautiful, isn't it?' he murmured softly.

'Yes! It is!' What was happening? It was taking
all her strength of will not to step back against
him and have him put his arms around her and
rest his chin lightly on the top of her head.

'Do you ever think about it, Charlotte?' he said
quietly.

'Think about what?' She said it almost carelessly; not thinking; not knowing what was coming next.

'Our marriage! Us!' He, too, was almost casual. 'Think about it and wonder what went wrong!'

'Nothing went wrong!' Instead of stepping back, she reached out and grabbed the balustrade. That, at least, was real; everything else was floating and a long way off. 'We were incompatible, that's all!' She daren't let herself consider. 'We should never have got married in the first place. We were just basically incompatible, that's all!'

'Not in all things as I remember!' His tone made her look round to find him watching her with an intensity that sent sparks leaping and igniting along her veins.

'No!' She fought the effect he was having on her. 'Maybe not! But sex isn't everything!'

'No,' he said, 'obviously not! Otherwise we would still be together!'

There was a long, long silence; in the moonlight, she could neither look at him, nor look away.

'It's strange, isn't it?' Now he was almost musing. 'The way fate has of bringing you back to face your greatest failure!'

'Is that what I was?' she said abruptly. 'Your greatest failure?'

'Maybe!' He smiled his glinting little smile. 'To date, anyway. I have no way of telling what the future's going to bring!'

'No,' she said. 'I see!' All she could see was Daniel. 'I'm sorry!'

'Don't be!' He was positive. 'It's probably just as well we went our separate ways!'

Another woman! A lot of them! Another wife! There was really no reason why she should have heard if he had married for a second time. Her mind thrashed round like a fish hooked on a line as she thought of a million reasons for what he had just said and she bit down hard on her cheek where the barb would be.

'Daniel, please!' Please what? Please tell me that there's no one else. Tell me that there have been others, if you like but please don't tell me that you're glad we went our separate ways because it gave you the opportunity to find somewhere else you could really love. She crumpled inwardly. 'Why are you doing this?'

'Because I want you to come back to me!' The world rocked on its axis and the night went dead. 'No!' He stopped her in mid-rush of breath. 'Let me finish what I have to say! God knows I've fought against it long enough!'

She wasn't fighting, she was feeling weak and the cold rail of the balustrade cut hard against her spine as she stepped back. At least that was real, and the stars and the moon and Daniel's face as the world began to revolve again.

'Last night,' he gave the reason for his visit to her room away, 'I came to talk to you and couldn't but now——!' He shrugged with his eyes never leaving hers. 'How long is it, Charlotte? Eight years?' It was almost ten since she had last heard that slight huskiness in his voice but eight since Daniel had agreed to their divorce; coming to America where such things were easier. 'Surely we should have changed in all that time?'

Oh, yes, she'd changed! She'd realised that ambition wasn't everything. She had made it to the very top—alone. Just as Daniel had always said she would but the aloneness she was now thinking of was quite a different beast.

'Maybe we have changed!' She said it reluctantly. 'But it's useless, Daniel. We can't go back!'

'Why?' To him, nothing was impossible. 'Why can't we go back and start again?'

Because she was frightened and afraid. Because she was . . . a million reasons presented themselves in her mind but the moonlight in Daniel's eyes was making her heart do crazy things and when he started to trace the outline of her chin and throat her mind went blank.

'You want me, I know that!' He paused with the knuckle of his forefinger softly against her jaw. 'Try and tell me that you don't!'

She couldn't answer and saw the gleam of victory in his face.

'There!' he whispered. 'There! You see!'

She could see nothing except his lips. 'It's too late!' She said it desperately.

'Is it?' He began to run his hands along her upper arms. She knew what he was doing but she couldn't stop him—or herself—as the space between them almost imperceptibly decreased. 'When I came down to San Francisco, that was what I thought! In fact, I didn't think at all! An actress had dropped out and I needed a replacement—quickly!' All the time that he was speaking, that space decreased. 'I knew you were available and I knew your work——!' She quickly looked up at him. 'I probably knew more about you and your work that I was willing to admit, even to myself!' he acknowledged with a rueful little smile. 'But when I came down to San Francisco, that was all it was going to be!' He went back to his main theme. 'A business trip to use whatever pressure I had to use to get you here but then I saw you!'

'And?' Now there was no space, just the full length of his body curved around her own. She didn't want to listen but she couldn't stop herself.

'And I realised that I'd let you waste ten years of our lives and that I couldn't let you go on doing it!' An almost frightening intensity had crept into his voice. 'You're staying here! That's right! Just here!' He caught her quick look down at his encircling arms. 'Until I hear you say you're going to give us a second chance!'

'I can't!' One failure: she had lived with that. A second would destroy her.

'Why not?' The fingers tightened and, like the jaw above her, the voice was razor sharp. 'Is there someone else? Calthrop?' He obviously found it difficult to say.

'No!' She pushed the thought of Bram almost guiltily to one side. 'Of course not!'

'In that case——' Daniel triumphant; Daniel watching her with his whole face alive. '——I can't think of anything that's stopping us, can you?'

'What are we going to do?'

'What do you mean?' Intent on tracing a line around her breast, Daniel didn't raise his head.

'Well, we'll have to tell them!' The bedroom was much larger than she had realised. Even in the dark, she could see how big it was.

'Tell them? Tell who?' His lips began to follow the line his finger drew.

'No! Daniel! Don't!' Carly sat up and pulled the sheet around her.

'Never?' He fought her with a laugh.

'No! Not never!' She also laughed and dug her fingers into crisp black hair to pull his head away. 'But not now!'

He lazily rolled over and grinned up at her, making a great show of looking at his watch. 'Then when?' he said.

'Daniel! You're impossible!' It had been wonderful. Back to the beginning but even better. Then—the first night of their honeymoon—she had been unsure. Not unsure of the incredible pleasure he had given her but of whether she was really pleasing him. But now? Could any man look at a woman just like that if his pleasure in her had not been just as great as hers in him.

'Okay—now who have we got to tell and what?' Daniel sat up against the pillows and slid an arm around her shoulders so that his hand could cup her breast.

She leaned into him. 'We have to tell the others!'

'What others?' He shot her a sidelong glance

through dark, spiked lashes, being deliberately obtuse.

'The cast! The members of the company!' She hissed and laughed her exasperation. 'The people at the theatre!' she said on a rising note. 'Everyone!'

'In that case,' he said comfortably, 'we'll take out an ad. in the local paper! To whom it may concern! Charlotte Mason has agreed to marry Daniel Stone—for the second time around!'

'But I haven't said I'll marry you!'

'No!' Now she had been the teasing one and he was serious. 'No,' he said, 'you haven't! But you will!' Deadly serious.

'And I suppose they're not expected to notice that we're living together until the advertisement comes out?' She tried to turn it into a joke. His intensity was almost frightening. 'At least,' it was the first time the thought had struck her, 'I assume you do want me to move in with you?'

'It's either that or I spend my time climbing up the drainpipe to your window!' In the semi-darkness of the bedroom his grey eyes glowed. 'And as for your concern about the others noticing, I'll work them so hard, they won't have time!'

'Be serious, Daniel! Daniel . . .!' Her voice faded to a sigh. His hand had moved and its urgency sent a kaleidoscope of colour spinning through her brain. How could she be expected to even think when Daniel was making love to her?

'Daniel!' This time it was lighter. Sunshine too

bright for the fabric of the curtains was filling every corner of the room. 'What *are* we going to do? I can't stop Angela and Cindy and they're bound to say something if I move out!'

'Okay!' His face was soft and heavy and relaxed. 'I'll call them all together when we get in and break the news! Which reminds me!' He had suddenly changed. One second, lying back against the pillows with his shoulder underneath her cheek; the next, swinging his feet on to the floor and twitching the sheet away from her. 'We've an hour to shower and dress and get to the theatre,' he informed her. 'I might be planning to get married——' with the light behind him, she felt his eyes rather than saw them travel over her, 'but I have no intention of letting that small fact make me late for work!'

CHAPTER SIX

'WE guessed it all the time, of course!'

'Guessed? Guessed what?' Carly was distracted. With Angela helping her to pack her things, it was taking twice as long.

'That you and Mr Stone were . . . well!' Angela shrugged and there was a wealth of meaning in that shrug. 'That there was something between you and Mr Stone!' she modified.

'Really?' Carly looked up. 'Pass me that skirt will you? And how did you know that?' It wasn't wise to be too curious but she couldn't stop herself.

'Sure! Here!' Angela passed the skirt across. 'Oh, I don't know!' She went back to her main topic. 'Something about the way he looked at you, I guess! And then, of course, he was up here the other night, wasn't he?' Angela finished, satisfied.

She didn't much like Angela, Carly decided. She would be a troublemaker if she got the chance. Although she had been pleased enough to have Carly make her peace for her with Daniel about the party, that wouldn't stop her spreading rumours or much worse.

No, she didn't like Angela Tilipski any more than she really cared for Polly Marshall, Carly decided.

'Clever!' That had been the word she had caught Polly mouthing across to Ed McMaster when Daniel had called not only cast but all the backstage staff together in the theatre first thing that morning.

'Ladies and gentlemen!' All eyes had turned to him. 'I have an announcement which for once has nothing to do with work!' There had been a few quickly hushed titters. 'I don't know how much of a surprise this may be to some of you but, in order to stop gossip and pointless rumour, I wanted you all to know that Miss Mason has done me the honour of agreeing to be my wife!'

She should have been thinking about Hollywood and her career as she stood there, beside Daniel, watching the way the light danced on his face and hair. Instead, she was thinking about babies—Daniel's babies—and what their life was going to be like. Hollywood belonged to a different person and so did a career once the next few months were over and Nina and Trelawney and the other parts she was due to play had become past history.

Charlotte! She heard her name in Daniel's resonant voice as someone asked him something. It was even a relief to be back to Charlotte and away from the trendy Carly. What had Daniel called it? A slick piece of public relations work designed for mass appeal! Carly smiled. From now on, she was going to be Charlotte—Charlotte Mason—the future Mrs Daniel Stone.

Hearing Daniel, standing there beside him, she

wasn't in the spotlight of harsh overhead working lights, she was in a rosy glow until, that was, she had caught sight of Polly Marshall and lip read the single word Polly had mouthed across to Ed McMaster.

'Clever!'

And, by Polly's standards, that must be exactly how she seemed. An unknown actress, out of nowhere, with two of the best parts of the season in her pocket and now the director. The last thing Polly would consider was that she might actually be in love with Daniel. For a person of Polly's stamp, love would be way down on the list.

The morning had been spoiled, almost the day and now, back in her narrow room that evening, packing, Angela was holding out a pair of shoes as if they were a weapon. 'Do you want these?' she said.

'Yes! Yes, thank you!' Carly took them. 'I think that's everything, don't you?'

Angela gave the narrow room a cursory glance. 'Seems like it!' Then, 'We'll miss you!'

Or her share of the rent. It was difficult to judge from Angela's tone of voice.

'I expect you'll manage!' Carly picked up her purse. There were still two months to go before what she had paid in advance, and insisted that they keep, ran out and, by that time, there might be someone else desperate to take her place.

'Your cab's here!' As they went through the door, Cindy's voice came floating up the stairs. Thank heaven for someone who was genuinely and uncomplicatedly pleased about what was happening.

After Daniel's general announcement, Cindy had come up to Carly and hugged her hard. 'I'm so pleased for you!' Cindy's elf-like face had glowed. 'We knew, of course!' It was to be the first of many times Carly was to hear those words. 'We knew there was *something* going on!'

But not that she and Daniel had been married once before. At the last moment, Carly had begged him not to tell them that.

'Are you having second thoughts?' Daniel had taken his attention from the road ahead just long enough to shoot her a quick hard glance.

'No, of course not!' Carly had run a hand through hair that the wind in the open sports car was tossing like a flag. 'It's just that . . .!'

That Polly Marshall walking studiously straight ahead across the theatre car park as if the sight of Daniel Stone and Charlotte Mason arriving for work together in his car was the most natural thing in the world, had quite enough grist for her gossip mill without the extra tantalising fact that Daniel Stone and Charlotte Mason had once been married—and divorced.

Polly Marshall and all the others for whom gossip and speculation was so much more interesting than plain, unvarnished truth.

'Okay! I understand!' Daniel had turned into his parking slot. 'But that's it! After this, no more secrets!'

'No, I promise!' Carly had answered fervently. 'None!'

So the whole cast knew that she was moving in with Daniel until pressure of work—particularly Daniel's—allowed them to take the time off to get married.

Thank goodness, at least in some ways, for some of the attitudes of theatre people. At least no one thought it odd or disapproved of what was happening, certainly not Cindy, half way up the stairs with Robin close behind her, leaning past to take the suitcase Carly was carrying.

Perhaps that was the reason for Angela's particular brand of sourness. Everyone was pairing off; everyone, that was, except Angela Tilipski.

'I would have thought Mr Stone would have come and got you, not let you go by taxi!' Angela remarked as Robin piled cases and the last few things stuffed into paper grocery bags into the trunk of the waiting cab.

'Not enough room!' Cindy supplied the answer for her. 'He drives a sports car, remember? He'd never get all this in that! Goodbye, Charlotte!' Suddenly Cindy's eyes were moist.

'Hey!' Resplendent tonight in a magenta satin shirt, Robin interrupted. 'She's just moving out, remember? Not going to the guillotine. This is a taxi, not a tumbril! You'll see her in the morning!' He put a satin arm around Cindy's waist and pulled her to him as he bent to give Carly's designation to the driver. 'The Tyler place!' he said.

'Goodbye! Take care!' Cindy with Robin's arm around her was the last thing Carly saw as the cab pulled away and drove off down the street.

She sat back in the corner and watched the world go by. First the stores and houses and then the almost park-like farm land with its big trees and green undulating fields. The lake wind usually dropped as the day got cooler and this evening was no exception; everything was quiet and still, even the black and white cows standing knee deep in the fields were motionless.

They might have been driven here by circumstance, but the people who had originally settled this community by the lake had chosen their spot well. What would they think of her moving in with Daniel? Carly caught herself smiling to herself. Probably disapprove.

Apart from the fact that they had come north during the American Revolution to stay under the British Crown, what she knew about the old United Empire Loyalists could have been written on the back of a very small postage stamp indeed. Presumably, however, if you were prepared to leave home and country for the sake of an ideal, you were equally highly principled about the sanctity of marriage!

Still, in a few months, she would be married and the old United Empire Loyalists could rest in peace. How strange life was! A month ago, her thoughts had all been of Hollywood and stardom and now Hollywood and stardom could belong to a different world.

She shifted restlessly against the cracked leather seat. Surely they should have been at the Tyler place by now? The journey hadn't seemed half as long when Daniel had been driving her.

At least they reached the drive and the cab turned into it but well before they reached the gleaming white façade of the house, she could see Daniel standing on the steps. Her heartbeat speeded up and her throat felt hollow.

It had been eight hours since she had seen him. They had switched to a rehearsal room after lunch for a read through of *Trelawney of the Wells* but Daniel had stayed behind in his office at the theatre, still trying to find a backer to replace the one who had dropped out. Without that backer, she had gathered, there would probably be no need for a read through of the play after *Trelawney of the Wells*. The season would probably collapse.

But the only strain in Daniel's face was of longing like her own when the cab drew up and he leaned down and opened the door for her.

'You didn't change your mind, then?' Grey eyes meshed with brown as she got out and the world, once more, stood still.

'No!' How could she? Standing there, looking up at him, how could she, even if she wanted to!

'That'll be ten dollars even!'

'What?' The world jolted on its way again as Daniel raised his head. 'What?' he said.

'The fare'll be ten dollars!' The cab driver repeated impatiently.

'Oh! Oh, yes!' Daniel put his hand in his pants pocket but Carly saw the expression on his face.

She laughed. 'It's okay! I'll pay!' At least some things never changed.

Daniel had never thought to check if he had

any money. She had lost count of the number of times she had gone running from their London flat to pay off cabs like this one, or else down to the little shop on the corner to settle for books and papers Daniel had brought home.

Daniel was successful and Daniel was well paid but Daniel never had a penny in his pocket. The one exception must have been the day they met. Then he had paid for the cab they shared to her front door.

'How did you ever manage to get along without me?' It was a joke as the cab went off along the drive.

But Daniel wasn't joking. 'I don't know,' he said abruptly, 'and I don't intend to try again. Now come on!' He took her arm and she saw the effort in his smile. 'Let's go inside. I don't want you getting any wrong ideas about who's in charge round here!'

As if she could. The only way she had been able to break the spell before had been to walk out on him and now fate had given her a second chance to walk back. On his terms—on any terms—just as long as she knew she would never have to face life without him again.

'I love you, Charlotte!' He pulled her to him with the urgency of raw longing the moment they got inside the door.

And I love you! Did she really need to say it? Surely he must see it written in her face and feel it in the body he held curved within his own.

'I'm sorry!'

It was a woman's voice and shock, like icy

fingers, ran down Carly's spine. They were alone here in this quiet house; why, then, was a woman walking across the hall from the direction of the still swinging door underneath the stairs? A woman with pale blonde hair and level cornflower eyes.

'I'm sorry!' She had a singsong voice. 'I did not know you were here!' And she looked less sorry than curious!

'Eva!' Daniel was clearly pleased to see her. 'Come and meet Charlotte! Charlotte Mason— meet Eva Jansen, my housekeeper!'

His housekeeper! Relief made her feel quite weak. The woman was his *housekeeper*! What had Daniel told her once? She came with the territory!

'I have left everything you asked for ready in the kitchen!' Around her, a conversation was going on. 'You are sure you do not want me to stay?'

'Quite sure!' Against her, Carly felt Daniel smile. 'I'm quite sure we can manage by ourselves!'

'In that case, I will go home!' There was a pause. 'Goodnight!' There was another pause. Eva Whoever-she-was who was not in love with Daniel any more than Daniel was in love with her, was waiting, Carly realised.

'Oh!' She felt and doubtless looked a fool. 'Oh, yes,' she said. 'Nice meeting you! Goodnight! But how's she going to get home?' The housekeeper was through the door before it dawned on her. It was a long way down the drive and then even longer along the road back into town. She knew; she had just driven it with every yard a mile and every mile eternity.

Distracted from his task of smoothing back her hair, Daniel smiled down at her. 'She doesn't,' he said blithely. 'She has her own apartment in the grounds—above the garage!'

'Oh, I see!' For some reason, Carly felt uneasy but——

'Come on!' Daniel dismissed the subject and propelled her towards the still swinging door underneath the stairs. 'You haven't got time to talk! You've got work to do!'

Work! Always before, in Daniel's terms, work had meant theatre but tonight it was cooking their own meal.

'Here!' He stood her in front of a bok choy cabbage and a Chinese cleaver ready on a block in the middle of the kitchen. 'Get chopping!' he instructed.

'But I can't!' Carly hefted the awkward weight of the sharp cleaver. 'I don't know how!'

'Then learn!' His fingers came down above hers, firm and warm. 'You've a lot of time!'

Was this really Daniel, this man smiling down at her with laughter lighting up his eyes and making his whole face come alive? It was. She didn't have to pinch herself. When he walked away across the kitchen, a part of her felt lost.

How many of the others would recognise Daniel Stone if they could see him now? She found herself wondering as she chopped, growing gradually more expert but still hearing Daniel working at a speed ten times faster than her own.

Some things about him would never change, of course. The mane of hair, still jet black with his back towards her and the way he stood, legs astride, weight balanced evenly, with the muscles in the backs of his calves and thighs pressing against the denim of his jeans.

But it was the concentration that was so much a part of him. She knew if she could see his face that the brows would be drawn together and the lips compressed in a straight line.

It had been this ability to concentrate that had been responsible for his success; that and a mind so brilliant that it could tie hers up in knots and leave her bleeding.

No, it was the surroundings that were different, not the man. The gleaming, ultra-modern kitchen, so out of tune with the rest of a house in which even the telephones were carefully antique. Just one or two rooms were out of character. This kitchen, the bathroom leading from their room——!

Their room! Carly caught herself and smiled. She had spent one night in it and already it was *theirs*.

'Finished?' Daniel turned towards her.

'Yes!' Suddenly she couldn't look at him. 'I think so!' She looked down at her roughly chopped bok choy instead.

'In that case,' a hand came out and swept the contents of the chopping block away, 'let's get it cooked!'

'I didn't know you could cook like this!'

'Really?' Across the table in the library, Daniel used chopsticks to pop a piece of shrimp into her mouth. 'I was forced to learn, remember?'

'Yes!' Her laugh seemed to come from someone else. It had happened once before, this feeling of being outside herself. She wanted him. She wanted him more than she had ever wanted anything in her life and yet she knew—this woman apart and slightly above herself—that something was waiting in the wings to intervene.

'Spaghetti and meat balls!' Daniel reminisced about the cause of some of their worst arguments. 'That's why I decided when you left——' he stopped with a tiny pulse beat leaping in his jaw. 'Well, let's just say,' he smiled and his face relaxed, 'that I decided I was more Chinese than Italian in my tastes!'

He could never be anything except Daniel and he could be everything if his taste included her.

'Do you want dessert?'

'No! No thank you!' She shook her head.

'And no coffee!'

'No!' He had remembered.

'Then, in that case!' Beyond the direction of his look, the lights marked a pathway to the door and then, beyond that, through the hall and up the stairs.

'But what about the dishes? Shouldn't we do them?' What was making her resist? She wanted above all things to follow that lighted pathway to the room above but something kept her rooted to her chair.

'I've no doubt Eva can take care of them in the morning!' Daniel was getting to his feet, slowly and smoothly with his eyes never leaving hers.

'Perhaps Eva won't want to!' Even her laugh was false. 'Perhaps she doesn't approve of me moving in with you!'

'Eva?' He snorted. 'At the moment, Eva's approval or otherwise is the last thing on my mind!' His voice dropped as he moved towards her. 'I want you, Charlotte——'

Want! She was doing it again. Standing outside herself and weighing and listening to everything he said. Want! Such a tiny word to mean so much.

'We've wasted so much time!' He was now behind her chair and her whole being reached up to him. 'Eight years! Ten! We'll never have those years again!' His hands moved down towards her shoulders and the breeze was cool on her heated skin as he lifted up the weight of hair and bent to kiss the tendrils clinging to her neck.

'No, please!' She wanted to—Oh, God! How she wanted to turn and bury herself against him in his arms—but a force beyond her ability to control kept her sitting there.

'Why? Are you frightened?' His voice was as soft as the breeze coming through the open windows.

Frightened! She clutched at the explanation like a drowning man. That must be it! The housekeeper's appearance had shaken her and she wasn't over it. Eva Whoever had a lot to answer for! It was so new, this new beginning—and so frightening.

This time, she let him draw her to her feet, seeking reassurance in his eyes.

'Don't be, my love!' She found her reassurance as he bent over her. 'We were meant to be together, you know that!'

At first his kiss was undemanding, just strong and sure against her lips but as her hands crept up against his shirt, his mouth began to move with a mounting pressure.

'Daniel!' It was a whisper deep inside her heart. 'Daniel!' This time it was louder but not so loud that she couldn't hear the blood racing in her veins or feel the crisp vibrance of the hair into which she convulsively dug her fingers.

The bedroom was too far away for the raging fire that suddenly consumed her. The couch was closer but how to tell him with her mouth hungrily searching his. But Daniel sensed it. Suddenly, from being on her feet with her body pressed against him, she was in his arms, weightless, with the movement of his chest against her as he carried her across the room.

Jet black on bronze. Nothing could change the darkness of Daniel's hair, certainly not the soft light beside the couch, but on her skin it had an easier task. Its quality gave it a burnished glow as Daniel's lips traced over it. Jet black on bronze; that was her last thought before the doorbell rang.

'Damn!' Daniel raised a face heavy with wanting her. Want! That one small word again but, this time, she shared the agony of frustration.

She sat up, fastening buttons that his urgent fingers had undone. 'Hadn't you better answer it?'

'No!' Daniel was adamant. 'Leave it! They'll go away!'

The doorbell rang again. 'It seems they won't!' If she had known, would she have been so calm? She even laughed as she looked up at him.

Daniel got slowly to his feet. 'Don't move!' he said. 'I'll deal with it!'

She had to move, of course. She had to stand and tuck her blouse into the waistband of her skirt so that when the door was opened and whoever was standing there could see through into the library-cum-lounge, she would be no more than a guest in Daniel's house.

Charlotte Mason. Actress! There could be any one of a million reasons why she was there.

At first it was only voices that she heard. Daniel's, a woman's and then another man. And still she didn't guess. Standing there, running her fingers through her hair, imagining the expression on her face and trying to adjust it; make it more neutral and more like that of a visitor.

'It's Polly!' All the time she had been trying to make herself seem quite at ease, a conversation had been going on and now Daniel was ushering two people into the room.

'Darling!' It *was* Polly. Full of the confidence of inside information, she walked straight ahead, leaving Daniel and the man beside him outside the circle of light thrown by the shaded lamps.

And *still* she didn't guess. What worried her

was Polly. Those shrewd almond eyes could see behind her efforts to seem quite casual. As for the man with Daniel, he was just a man. As tall, perhaps, but a little diffident in the half tone light.

'When he said it was important, I thought I'd better bring him here!' Polly went rattling on with an explanation. 'We did try calling but there was no reply!'

The telephone! At one point, Carly had heard it ring but, lost in Daniel, the sound had seemed to be coming from another world.

'But I knew you must be here!' Oh, yes, Polly knew. One look at the satisfaction on her face was proof of that. 'So I thought, why not bring him down!'

How strange it was—even knowing that Polly was savouring the suspense of what she had really come to say, could not stop the thought passing through Carly's mind. The place where you were living was always up and the place you were going was always down. Polly had come *down* from the theatre to break whatever news it was she had to break even though the house they were all now in was several hundred feet higher than the theatre beside the lake.

'Do come in!' Daniel was ignored. Polly's invitation was to the man standing at his side. 'I told you she would be here!' Even Polly was not quite immune. Her voice broke and then escalated to a feverish laugh as Daniel shifted slightly and looked in her direction. 'Darling!' She acknowledged him. 'I was sure you wouldn't mind! Not when he said he was a friend of Charlotte's and not when you hear what he's come to say!'

'And exactly what is that?' Carly heard the cutting edge to Daniel's voice and perhaps, at last, she guessed.

'Why don't you let him tell you, darling?' The girlish act just didn't work but Polly was obviously uncomfortable.

'Why not indeed!' Daniel's voice was dry and Daniel was once more in control.

Carly shivered. Daniel had no need to step back. She knew the man in the doorway must be Bram.

CHAPTER SEVEN

OUTWARDLY, everything stayed just the same. Charlotte Mason was still going to marry Daniel Stone and, until that 'happy event' could take place, they would go on sharing this big house on the hill. It was underneath the surface, where it mattered most, that things had changed. There was going to be no marriage and Carly knew it from the moment Bram walked across and took her hand in both of is.

'Carly!' He was a little like Daniel, Carly realised except that where Daniel's colours were bold and strong, Bram's were paler. Brown hair instead of black; pale blue eyes instead of turbulent, ever-changing grey and a skin that was pallid, without Daniel's sheen of bronze. But otherwise, there was a similarity, not just of stamp and build but in the almost English accent of the voice. Bram's eyes studied her without expression in his smiling face. 'I hope this isn't inconvenient,' he said.

'No! No, of course not!' She wished he wouldn't hold her hand quite so possessively. 'How are you, Bram?' She made an effort. What was happening was hardly Bram's fault. If there was any ulterior motive in coming here, it lay with Polly. She could see the expression on Polly's face as she stood expectantly slightly to one side, waiting to find out what was going to happen next. She could also see the ice cold set of Daniel's as he stood next to Polly.

'I'm fine!' Bram went on smiling, apparently totally unaware of the conflicting currents in the atmosphere. 'One hundred per cent fit again, or so my doctors say!'

And he looked it. He had even put on a little weight during his convalescence and it suited him. It gave him a substance he had previously lacked and fleshed out his tall, slightly angular frame. He now looked exactly what he was. Brampton Calthrop III, old money Boston millionaire and business man.

'I've been expecting to hear from you!' Was he quite so unaware of what was happening? Carly wondered as he spoke.

'Yes, I'm sorry!' She felt uncomfortable. Bram had, after all, been good to her. In a way, he was responsible for her being here even though, when she had seen him lying underneath that truck, she had thought her career had come abruptly to an end. 'I did try calling you,' she said it too anxiously and caught the hard reaction on Daniel's face. 'But no one would put me through!'

'Yes! I heard!' Why wouldn't he stop smiling and let go of her hand?

'I thought you were still in Boston!' She said it to break an awkward silence.

'I escaped last week!' Bram answered smoothly. 'Back to New York! You remember the apartment?'

'Yes!' She did. She had been there once. A big spacious place with a view of Central Park. His home away from home, away from the all seeing eyes of his mother and his sister. Carly remembered thinking how strange it was that a man of fifty needed to carry on such a subterfuge—surely he should have been able to break away from the apron strings by now—but that was Bram, she had suddenly realised. Devoted son and brother on the outside but quite different underneath.

She had always avoided paying a second visit to that apartment but Daniel could not know that. Daniel could only know what he was hearing. That she was obviously quite familiar with Bram's New York home.

She managed at last to free her hand from Bram's only to have him look down, then up again with one of his bland smiles. 'I hear congratulations are in order!' he said in his smooth voice. 'Or,' for the first time the conversation included Daniel, 'is it the prospective groom one congratulates on such occasions?' He *was* enjoying it. In lieu of a reply he bent and kissed Carly on the cheek. 'Congratulations—and congratulations, Stone!' He slowly straightened with his eyes never leaving hers. 'You're a very lucky man!'

'I'm sure I am!' Lucky to have found out just in time; lucky to have an excuse for calling the marriage off? Carly wondered which sort of luck Daniel had in mind. It was certainly not the sort Bram had been talking about.

'Anyway!' Polly burst in. 'You haven't heard why Mr Calthrop's here!'

'No!' He hadn't heard, he'd guessed. Two strings to her bow; two men not just willing but able to further her career and no particular scruples about how either one of them was used. Which particular conclusion was Daniel drawing behind that one curt syllable?

'You'll love it when you know!' Love! She had never even told Daniel that she loved him! In her head and heart all the time he had been holding her but she had never put it into words. It was Polly rattling on but Carly thinking.

Polly came across and took Bram's arm; some acquaintances were obviously meant to ripen rapidly. Polly would have absolutely no objection to becoming Mrs Brampton Calthrop III. In her own words, it would be a 'clever' move. 'Mr Calthrop's going to underwrite the season!' Polly broke their news breathlessly. 'Go on, darling, tell him!' she urged Bram.

'I heard one of your backers had dropped out!'

It was going to be all right. Listening to Bram's dry, rather drawling voice, Carly knew that the worst five minutes of her life were over and that everything was going to be all right. Bram wasn't here in pursuit of her, he was here to offer the huge sum of money needed for the season to continue and of course Daniel would understand. Daniel was the last person to confuse survival with sentiment.

It might not be entirely coincidence that Bram had chosen this particular cause for his largesse—

he had, after all, known exactly where she was—
but it had been Daniel who had spent hours
contacting the money markets of the world
searching for a backer to replace the one who had
dropped out. And Bram had heard. He had been
in New York and he had just heard.

Carly felt ridiculously light headed. It was
going to be all right.

'I'll have my accountants call yours in the
morning and draw the agreement up!'

Around her, Bram's conversation with Daniel
was coming to an end.

'Yes, do that!' Daniel inclined his head. 'You'll
be flying back to New York, I suppose?'

'No!' It wasn't going to be all right. Her
optimism had been premature and foolish. She
sensed it as Bram began. 'I thought I might stay
on here for a few days. My diary's empty
and——' his glance washed over her, '—I've
always had rather a fondness for the theatre!'

'Really?' Daniel answered drily. 'In that case,
you must look in on a few rehearsals!'

'I'd be delighted!' Bram could not have been
more charmed or charming. 'And now there's
just the question of accommodation . . .!'

He could have her old narrow room, Carly
found herself thinking almost hysterically, unless,
of course, she would need that room herself.

'I think the King Edward, don't you, darling?'
Polly came forward and took Bram's arm and,
this time, the darling was to Daniel.

Poor Polly! She was going to have to work a
good deal harder than she already was if she

wanted to catch Bram, but then Polly didn't know that Bram wasn't here to back a season. He was here to enforce a contract that had already been drawn up—a much more personal contract.

Carly remembered the planned drive across the States from San Francisco and its hidden implications. Bram's accident had stopped the trip taking place but Bram had spent a lot of money on sponsoring her career—if it hadn't been for him she would never have got the showcase part which had led to Daniel asking her to work for him—and now Bram wanted payment.

She knew it, Bram knew it and—she shot him a nervous glance—so did Daniel.

'Why not?' This time, Daniel's drawl was obvious. 'I believe the King Edward's a first class hotel. It's central, near the theatre. I'm sure you'll find it has everything you need!'

Like a discreet night porter! Carly burned at the implication implicit in his voice but Polly gushed. 'There you are, then! That's all settled!' She put her other hand over the one she had slipped through Bram's arm and linked them together. 'I'll drive you!'

'No, really!' Bram demurred. 'I'll get a cab!'

'Why not?' Polly's insistence was almost embarrassing. 'I brought you here, didn't I? It's only fair that I should take you back! Besides,' if a woman of Polly's type could snuggle, Polly snuggled closer, 'it'll give us more of a chance to get to know each other!'

'How very kind!' Bram disengaged her fingers and Carly found herself with her hand in his.

'Goodnight, my dear!' It was just too personal; just too much of a reminder of how awkward she had always been when she had been forced to walk part-dressed in front of him in her dressing room. 'And goodnight, Stone!' Bram went on watching her. 'Once again,' his grip relaxed and Carly snatched her hand away, 'congratulations! You're a very lucky man!'

Daniel saw them out but she stayed standing there, trying false hope to reassure herself, trying anything. She would explain—not that there was anything to explain, of course. And *of course* Daniel woud understand.

In a few moments, he would be back and they would be laughing about the coincidence that had brought Bram back into her life—and about Polly's too obvious eagerness—and then they would go upstairs and things between them would be as they had always been meant to be.

'So!' There was no hope, no hope at all. The skin on Daniel's face was stretched against the bone and his eyes were glittering as he came back through the door. 'Who do I congratulate, I wonder? You or myself?' He saw her puzzlement. 'You for proving whatever it was you had to prove or me for finding out before I made a complete fool of myself!' he elaborated cynically.

'Daniel!' But he had turned away towards the decanter on the buffet and all she could see was the hunched set of his shoulders and the anger in his spine. 'Darling, please! What's wrong? I can explain!'

He turned on her and her outstretched hand

fell limply to her side. 'What's wrong?' he jibed. 'Nothing, I would imagine, as far as you're concerned!' To anyone who didn't know him well, he would just be angry. She, however, knew him well enough to sense how near the fine edge of control he really was. The voice might have that icy quality of calm control but the tiny muscles round his mouth were quivering and the liquor shivered in his glass. 'You have what, Charlotte,' he went on in that smoothly deceptive voice. 'An ex-husband who can't wait to marry you and a lover who is presumably in exactly the same boat! Congratulations, Charlotte!' He parodied Bram's word. 'I hadn't realised what a very fine actress you really are!'

She shook her head in a gesture of despair. 'But I didn't know Bram was coming here! Daniel, be reasonable——!' She had almost gone too far. The liquor in the tumbler jumped and the muscles around his mouth jerked convulsively. 'How could I?' she said more calmly. 'The other backer only fell out a few days ago. How could I have known that Bram was going to take his place?'

'Doesn't he always buy everything you want?' Daniel flashed back viciously. 'Now he's bought you a theatre—or at least a part of it! And I've no doubt you'll be duly grateful, or at least express your gratitude in the old, time honoured way!'

He halved his drink with his eyes never leaving her.

'One day, you know,' he was now almost conversational, 'you really must try and stand or fall on your abilities as an actress and not your abilities in bed. You're really quite good, you know!' This time, the glass was emptied. 'Or have I already told you that?'

'Daniel! Listen! Please!' She was desperate. 'You heard Bram! He was pleased we're getting married! We were friends, that's all, just——' Why, of all times, did her breathing have to let her down? 'Just friends!' she finished. She didn't even convince herself.

'Just *good* friends is, I think, the proper term!' Daniel retorted cynically. 'And you're right!' For a moment, his sudden change of attack was baffling. 'I did hear Calthrop congratulating us. The only trouble is, I also saw his face. He was amused, Charlotte, and I wonder why? Had you had some sort of bet with him or was it entirely your own idea? Carly Mason is going to marry Daniel Stone!' In his mouth, the trendy version of her name was an obscenity. 'Encourage him with a little competition, was that it?' He taunted her with the question mark of his bitter smile. 'Unless, of course, Brampton Calthrop, like the U.S. cavalry, finds some excuse to gallop to the rescue in the nick of time! Oh, don't worry, Charlotte, I believe you!' A sudden hope flared and died. 'I don't think even you—or Calthrop—had anything to do with our previous backer dropping out!'

He turned away, leaving her defeated. She knew that particular tone of voice. He had used it so many times to end one of their furious arguments. Then, the cause had always been her career and she had been the one who had been accusing him of not loving her. Now, he was in the wrong—not that it really mattered. Carly watched him as he went across the room, older even than she felt with every grey hair showing and shoulders hunched in the bitterness of defeat.

In his list of reasons for their marriage going sour, Daniel had left out one thing. Communication! Perhaps communication was something they both still had to learn. If only she could go to him, rest her head against his back and find the words to tell him what the truth really was but—looking at that back, marshalling her own feeble skill with words, she knew it was impossible. She had no talent and Daniel had no wish to hear.

She turned and went towards the telephone.

'What are you doing?' Daniel heard the slight sound as she picked it up.

'Calling a cab!' She mechanically began to dial. 'To take me back to Cindy and Angela's house!'

'You'll do no such thing!' It was odd how some things never changed. The pressure of his fingers on her hand could still speed up the beating of her heart. 'You're staying here—with me!'

'Why?' she said. Her bones felt brittle as she raised her face to his. 'You don't want me here!'

'No!' So much for hope, however foolish and misplaced. 'No,' he said, 'I don't! But here is exactly where you're going to stay!'

'Then I'll leave tomorrow!' She was too tired to fight.

'You'll leave when the season finishes and not before!'

For a moment she was afraid. This was a Daniel she had never really seen. Angry but more than angry as his eyes bored into her.

'We're going to get married, remember, Charlotte, and until the season ends, that's exactly what the situation is. I won't have you undermine my authority with the company by making a fool of me—not publicly, at least! Do what you like with Calthrop!' His whole face was a sneer. 'I'm sure discretion is a virtue that he values, anyway! But while you're here,' he dropped the twisted mask of comedy, 'you will—as far as everyone except Calthrop is concerned—live with me!'

'And then?' Tired or not, she challenged him.

'And then the company breaks up and you do exactly what you like!'

'I see!'

'Oh, don't worry!' He caught her upward look. 'We're well equipped with bedrooms. I think this house has five!'

'I hate you, Daniel!' How often had she thought it—now it was out in words.

'Really?' Dark eyebrows lifted above his question mark of a smile. 'Then it's just as well you discovered it before we made a second attempt to ruin both our lives!'

He walked out through the door and she heard him go upstairs. One, two, three, four, five—he had walked right round the upstairs landing, past the room they had once shared. She heard a door slam right at the very end. Daniel had obviously decided to leave her the room with the memories.

Slowly and dispiritedly she followed him up the stairs, flicking off light switches as she went, but the house had been in darkness for several hours before she got to sleep and, when she woke, it wasn't sunshine filtering through the curtains that had aroused her but the persistent sound of rain driving hard against the windows.

She showered and dressed in jeans and shirt and pulled her hair tightly back in a pony tail. Sometimes, at least, the weather matched your mood. The view outside the window had been transformed overnight. No longer lush green parkland, the grass was sodden and windswept and the dripping trees stood in the circles of their own blossom which the wind had ripped off.

She picked up her tote and her *Trelawney* script and went downstairs, turning left at the bottom, away from the library and walking across the black and white tiled floor of the hall towards the swing door leading to the kitchen. Daniel was standing with his back to her.

'Good morning!' She had to lick her lips to say it.

'Good morning!' Daniel didn't turn. He was also dressed in jeans and shirt but they were much darker than her own and she could see the rigid tension of his muscles through the fabric. 'There's coffee in the pot!' he said abruptly.

'Thank you!' She went across and poured and wrapped her fingers gratefully around the china mug. The room was cold—unless, that was, it was the cold deep in her bones that was making her so chilly.

Daniel had moved, she noticed. Not much but just enough to make sure that, when she went across to the coffee pot on the counter, there would be no accidental contact.

She stood there watching him through lowered lashes; head thrust forward, shoulders hunched, watching the rain coming down against the window. The silence was intense and she cast round desperately for a remark to break it but everything that came to mind was either too trivial or too important to entrust to words which might be misunderstood.

'Eight-thirty!' The sound of Daniel's voice and his coffee mug going down on the counter was enough to make her jump. 'Do you want me to drive you to the theatre!'

'No!' His indifference was crushing. 'I'll get a cab. I'm not called until ten!' He began to turn away and she couldn't bear it. She couldn't let things end like this. 'Daniel!' Her hand went out.

'Yes?' He turned and her hand dropped to her side. His face was shocking; in one night, he seemed to have aged ten years. 'Yes?' he repeated curtly. 'What do you want?'

I want to get behind that mask with the burning eyes and try something—somehow—to get you to understand. I didn't ask Bram here. I had no idea he was coming and he means nothing—*nothing!*—to me compared with you. In fact, it's hard to think of anything that has really been important in the last ten years—not even the career which I once thought meant so much.

'What is it, Charlotte? What do you want?' Daniel overrode her thoughts. 'I don't have time for playing games!'

'Nothing!' Her voice was dull. 'I'm sorry! It doesn't matter!'

What was the point? Daniel was not going to believe her—could she really think he would as she watched him go? As far as Daniel was concerned, she had never broken up with Bram. Bram had always been going to follow her to Canada and continue what had probably been a long-standing affair. And, as far as the opportunity to save the theatre was concerned, that was just the last turn of the screw. Daniel was now beholden to Brampton Calthrop—lover and maybe future husband of his ex-wife.

Carly mechanically stacked the dirty coffee mugs into the dishwasher. God, what a mess! She looked around the immaculate, shining kitchen. God, what an awful mess!

Eva arrived before she left and then the cab came that she had called. She supposed she must have behaved quite normally because no one looked at her as if she was being strange but nothing was quite real until she was sitting in the rehearsal room with the *Trelawney* script in front of her and she heard her name.

'Hallo, Carly!'

She looked up. 'Bram?' she said questioningly.

He smiled. 'Why the surprise? Stone said I could look in on rehearsals if I liked, remember?

Do you mind if I sit down?' He nodded towards the wooden chair across the table.

'No! No, of course not!' What more could the sight of Charlotte Mason having an intimate little *tête à tête* with Brampton Calthrop possibly lose her?

Besides, there was no one there to see. They were using one of the rehearsal rooms this morning while the theatre stage was set and lit for the Chekhov and, like most small town parish halls, it had one big hall for major functions and several little side rooms. They were still walking through *Trelawney* and Carly had taken refuge in one of the little side rooms while she waited for her call.

She could hear the others through the open doorway and, anyway, the ASM would come and call her when Harley was ready for her.

That had been the first news of the morning and it had come from an overly confidential Polly. Harley, she said portentously, had been promoted. Daniel had dropped by first thing and announced that pressure of all his other work had made it necessary for him to step down from *Trelawney* and that Harley would be taking his place as director. It was a big boost for Harley—this promotion from assistant to associate director—and he was making the most of it, judging from the self important way he was now behaving.

Daniel's announcement had come as a big surprise, Polly had confided with a gleam in her almond eyes. He had always seemed so on top of things; taking everything that was thrown at him in his stride. It must, Polly had said slyly, be the strain of mixing all the responsibility for the season with his personal life. Carly, too, she added, was also looking a touch tired.

'So!' It was Bram now studying her across the table with a knowing look in his pale blue eyes. 'You're getting married!'

'Yes!' She blurted it. 'I'm sorry, Bram!' Now why had she said that. She had absolutely no need to apologise. Bram had never asked her and there had never been any agreement that she would marry him; just an arrangement that the two of them, alone together, would take a slow drive through the States from San Francisco to New York.

'Don't be!' Bram was just too urbane. 'It's not myself I'm thinking of, it's you! You know, of course, you're making a terrible mistake!'

She was making nothing—the irony hit her hard—but, 'I obviously don't think so!' For Daniel's sake, the show had to go on. She even raised a little smile.

'Obviously not, otherwise you wouldn't be doing it!' Urbane, charming, Ivy League, a scene of any sort would be anathema to Bram but there was a cutting edge behind the quiet remark.

She was seeing the other side of Bram. The side which ruled a financial empire and stood behind political thrones and that sort of power and influence was not achieved—and most certainly not held—on the basis of charm and urbanity alone.

Looking at that quietly smiling face, she shivered. What had she once called Daniel? Emperor Stone! The title fitted Daniel but it also fitted Bram and she had thought—No! She hadn't even thought. She had just fallen headlong back in love with Daniel and assumed that Bram would quietly fade away. Bram had invested thousands—perhaps hundreds of thousands—in promoting her career and she had let him without once considering there was bound to be a day of reckoning.

She hadn't thought! That should be her epitaph. She just hadn't thought!

'I'm sorry!' That meaningless phrase again. 'I'm fond of you, you know that, and I'm grateful, I really am but . . .!' She spread her hands and looked down at them.

'You know, you disappoint me, Carly!' He could have been talking about the weather for all the colour in his voice. 'I would have thought you were much too intelligent to make the same mistake a second time around!'

'What?' She faced him with her heart thudding in her chest.

'My dear Carly, you don't think I haven't made a few enquiries?' Using the network of contacts and employees that had once come up with the name he was using so casually. 'Of course I know—have known for a long time—that you and Stone were married!'

'I see!' Her voice was dull. 'Who have you told?'

'No one!' Bram was amused. 'Why should I? What's in the past is between you and Stone!'

'And the future?' The word hung in the air. She had no need to feel loyal but there was much more depending on his answer than Daniel's self esteem. Her personal life was very much tied up with the future of the theatre. The percentage Bram had invested was quite small compared with the whole but it held the balance and if Bram withdrew, as his unknown predecessor had so unexpectedly done, it might be too late for even Daniel to find the money for even this first season to continue.

She wasn't going to marry Daniel Stone and Bram had no need to be concerned but she couldn't tell him. . . . Loyalty, again. Loyalty to Daniel and not making a fool of him!—and there was no telling what Bram might do.

'My dear, Carly!' He misread her horrified expression with a smile. 'You really haven't changed too much, have you? First and always, your career! But you needn't worry! I'm not going to withdraw! I've more than one interest in seeing this season comes safely to an end!'

An interest in his investment and an interest in her. He didn't have to spell it out as he sat there watching her with all the confidence of a man who always wins in his pale blue eyes.

'Charlotte!' The voice came from behind her and Carly spun round in her chair. Why, of all people, had it had to be Polly who had come in just then. A child could sense the tension in the atmosphere and, far from a child, Polly was a shrewd scheming woman with a fine eye for scandal. 'I'm sorry if I'm interrupting anything!'

Her eyes flicked back and forth. 'But we're ready for you, Charlotte. The ASM was busy so I said I'd give you your call!' She had probably been only too pleased to volunteer and have the opportunity of finding out exactly what was happening between the theatre's newest backer and one of its female leads. Well, she hadn't found out everything but at least she had something to report. 'They were gazing at each other, darlings! Eating each other up! Poor Daniel! I wonder if he knows!'

'Why don't you come and watch!' Imagining Polly's comments, it came as something of a shock to hear her real voice floating past her head. 'We're just about to read through Charlotte's big scene,' Polly went on to Bram. 'I'm sure you'd find *that* interesting!'

CHAPTER EIGHT

SHE gave what must have been the worst performance of her life. Even allowing for the fact that this was just a walk through of *Trelawney of the Wells*, plotting moves and lines and that, like her, most of the cast were carrying and still relying heavily on their scripts, her interpretation was abysmal. She was once more playing a young girl but she was leaden. A rank amateur could have done better.

At the end of an unending day, Harley looked up from a conversation with Polly and Ed McMaster. 'Miss Mason, Mr McMaster and Miss Marshall!' Flushed with his new importance, Harley was copying Daniel in using proper names. 'The rest of you can break until tomorrow—notes at nine!—but I would like Miss Marshall, Miss Mason and Mr McMaster to stay on, please!'

Carly stood and watched as everyone except the three of them and Harley and the ASM picked up scripts and jackets and went off laughing and chattering through the outside door. There were one or two backward glances in her direction but that was all.

'Oh! And Helen! Perhaps you'd stay, too!' At the last minute, Harley stopped the girl who was Carly's understudy and playing a very small part.

'If you don't mind!' Harley was positively bending over backwards with his courtesy.

The girl coloured. 'No, of course not!' She was positively breathless with not minding.

If you were an understudy and you were kept behind, it could only mean one thing. A chance of taking over the actual part. And Carly could hardly blame their new director for thinking along those lines. If she went on as she was—faltering, stumbling, wooden—she would ruin Harley's very first production on his own.

Poor Harley! Standing in the background like the class dunce kept in after school, she found it in her heart to be sorry for him. Not only was his own career on the line but he was having to face the fact that he might be going to have to replace the actress who was going to marry Daniel Stone!

Poor Harley! If only he knew that one, at least, of his many problems did not exist. She wasn't going to marry Daniel even though keeping up that charade until the season ended was going to be the most difficult performance of her life.

She stood there watching him talk to Ed and Polly and guessing at the whispered conversation. He knew it was an imposition for actors of their experience but would they mind—would they possibly mind—staying on and running through a few of the *Trelawney* scenes again in the hope Miss Mason might just get the feel of them?

Helen—Anderson? Williamson? Carly found she didn't know, although the fair haired girl had certainly been one of the many visitors to the narrow house—was sufficiently unimportant in the overall scheme of things just to be asked to stay but Polly and Ed McMaster had egos that must be stroked.

'I hardly think we need keep Miss er ...!' Bram's voice as the whispered conversation came to an end, startled her. He had been there all day; a Grey Eminence in the shadows on one of the chairs pushed back against the wall. Bram, too, had no idea of Helen's name but there was no mistaking the wealth of meaning as he looked at her. 'I'm sure this young lady has something better to do with her evening than stay here watching scenes she's already seen half a dozen times today!'

'Oh!' For a second, Harley looked nonplussed. Another choice to make; this time between what he wanted and the wishes of an important backer. 'Oh, yes ... well ... er ... maybe you're right, Mr Calthrop!' Harley backed down. He might be standing in Daniel's shoes, but Harley was no Daniel. 'It's okay, Helen!' he said to the crushed girl. 'You can go, after all!'

'Don't let him keep you here too long! You're looking tired!' Bram moved across to Carly, protecting his investment. Not the obvious one of the production but the moral obligation of the investment he had already made in her. And now she was even more indebted. However good or bad she was, there was to be no understudy taking over in *Trelawney of the Wells*. 'Besides, I've got other ideas for our evening, too!' Carly saw Polly look daggers as Bram ran his hand along her arm. 'I thought we might go out to dinner. I'm told the food at the King Edward's very good!'

'I'm not sure if Daniel's free!' Carly fell back on the charade.

'In that case, come alone! If, that is, your fiancé has no objection? Would you like me to call him?' Bram was all smoothness as he turned towards the telephone on the wall.

'No!' The last thing she wanted was for Bram and Daniel to have a conversation. 'No!' She toned her much too fierce reaction down. 'I'm sure Daniel won't have any objection. Thank you!'

'Good!' His eyes slid over her. 'In that case, shall we say the King Edward at eight o'clock!'

'Yes,' she muttered. 'That'll be fine!'

With a last word to the others, Bram walked out of the rehearsal room. It was all quite simple really. Bram had got exactly what he wanted and she had been manipulated by a master.

'Okay, everyone!' Harley made an effort to upstage Bram in everybody's minds. 'Let's get started. Miss Mason over there!' He directed her to the tape line on the floor marking the place where the window of the actual set would be. 'Mr Mason right of centre in his wheelchair and Miss Marshall ready for her cue!'

The scene started and this time, Carly sought and found her concentration. Trelawney was her part and she was going to keep it. And not because of any influence—on her own merits!

When Harley finally released them and she got home, the house was empty and she kept the cab outside. It shouldn't take her much more than ten

minutes to shower and change and keeping the
meter ticking was cheaper than calling another
cab from town.

She hurried with her dressing. Olive skin could
manage without make-up and, as for her hair,
that could go from just being scraped back in a
pony tail to being put up in a simple knot. A
white dress—No! She picked it out and promptly
put it back. Apart from all its associations with a
wedding, white was too striking with her dark
skin and hair. It might look as if she was trying to
make an impression and that was the last idea she
wanted Bram to get. Especially as the last thing
she wanted was to go out with him at all.

God, what a mess! She meant her life but when
she looked around her room, unlike the gleaming
kitchen, this time the silent comment fitted.
Clothes torn off and dumped half on the bed and
half on the floor, sneakers underneath the
dressing table and the closet doors both open
with the clothes pushed hurried along the rail.
Her clothes and—her breath was painful—some
of Daniel's.

Daniel! She thrust bare feet awkwardly into
high heeled, strappy sandals. She had promised
herself she wouldn't think of Daniel and where
he was and what he might be doing. The only
thing that mattered was that he wasn't with her
and never would be—now. How long would it
take the news of her intimate little dinner with
Bram to reach him, she wondered briefly. Not
long, judging by the expression on Polly's face
when she had left rehearsal.

Comb, change purse—she checked her blue suede clutch purse. Perfume—her finger went automatically to the spray before she realised what she was doing. The seductive fragrance drifted round the room. Oh, well, what was a little perfume? Hardly the signal for the big seduction. But she left the cut glass bottle on the dressing table as she checked the other small items in her purse.

Not quite fifteen minutes! She stood up and checked her wristwatch. She had done well. She had been in the same room with the bed she had once shared with Daniel for almost fifteen minutes and she had managed to think of him only once.

With a last look in the mirror, she almost ran out of the door and down the curving staircase only to come face to face with Daniel when she reached the bottom stair.

'Most attractive!' He surveyed her in the blue dress she had finally picked out and his drawl reflected the cynicism in his eyes as he smelled the perfume in the air. 'What is it?' he asked wryly. '*Joy* or *Vent Verte*?'

'*Joy!*' Nothing was going to go her way tonight. Not even a thoughtless use of perfume.

'How very appropriate!' he drawled. 'Appropriate, that is, for the evening you no doubt have in mind!'

He must have been in the house all the time. At least, the door into the library was open and she could see a light. Daniel also had a script in one hand; probably the new Bosworth play which was due to be the third production of the season.

'I've no particular sort of evening in mind!' She found herself watching the movement of his chest; slow and even, evidence of strict control. 'I'm——' she gave a nervous little shrug, 'just going into town!'

'In fact, you're going out to dinner!' he informed her coolly. 'With Calthrop!'

Her eyes leaped up. In the angle of his jaw, a pulse was beating.

'Yes!' There was a telephone in the library. Lucky Polly! It had probably taken her just the one call to locate him. 'Why not?' Defeat gave her the courage of bravado. 'Oh, don't worry, I didn't tell him anything! He even invited you but I said——' she was forced to look away around the hall, '—I said I didn't think you could come!' she finished lamely.

'How very discreet of you—and loyal!' Above a twisted mouth, two grey eyes taunted.

'Yes,' she said, 'it was!'

'Oh, come now, Carly!' He made the shortened version of her name an insult. 'Don't take me for an utter fool! Do you really expect me to believe that Calthrop doesn't know *exactly* how things stand between us? How, I wonder, did you put it? Too much wine one evening, or was an irresistible rush of nostalgia to the brain responsible for you agreeing to marry me again?'

'Daniel, you've got to listen——!'

But he was in no listening mood. 'Anyway, whatever explanation you dreamed up, I'm quite sure it was convincing! What did you say, I wonder? That having given in to this moment of sheer madness, you now feel some obligation to save *poor* Daniel's face? So, if darling Bram has no objection,' he mimicked her savagely, 'you'll stay here for the duration of the season——' Here! In this house, aware of Daniel every second. 'And, in return, you'll make sure his director doesn't walk out on him! Was that how you put it, Charlotte?' He seared her with his look. 'For the price of a little trust, both of Calthrop's investments can be protected!'

'That's not true!' She was desperate. 'You're twisting everything!'

'Am I?' he said coolly. 'And am I also twisting your reason for coming back to me? It was a way of paying an old score, wasn't it, Charlotte? Ten years ago, you left me and now, to make your point, you had to have me begging you to come back. I'm sorry it took so long and that making your point has created so many complications in your life, but then Calthrop understands! We've already established that!'

She was frightened, really frightened as he looked at her. No one had ever hated her so much.

'He must do!' Point, counter-point; she could feel his fury but his voice was icy calm. 'Otherwise why should he agree to this more than bizarre arrangement? How tolerant is he, Charlotte?' He was even conversational. 'Does he know that I've made love to you?'

'No!' She said it dully.

'In that case, you *were* discreet!' he drawled.

'Because I don't think even a man of Calthrop's stamp could be that tolerant!'

'Excuse me!' Why was she even trying to get him to understand. Daniel's mind was brilliant but, at the moment, it was closed. 'I have a taxi waiting!'

'I'm sorry!' He stepped back with an elaborate courtesy. 'I didn't realise I was keeping Calthrop waiting. I wish you joy!' The perfume was suddenly overpowering. 'Do I wait up for you— or not?'

She went straight past him and out to the waiting cab.

'The King Edward!' It was a relief to make a statement that could be neither misconstrued nor misunderstood. Carly gave the instruction to the driver and settled back in her seat, thinking of nothing except the scenery as the cab gathered speed and went along the drive. But her few seconds' respite from reality were like fool's gold. She had to decide, and quickly, what she was going to say to Bram.

Bram was waiting in the doorway to the bar. 'My dear, you look ravishing!' His eyes ranged over her.

Dull blue and black! She had never liked the dress she had hastily picked out and had no idea why she had bought it except that the sales clerk had been so pushing, she would have almost bought anything just to get out of the store. But the blue did nothing for her except make her skin look sallow against the darkness of her hair; the length was wrong and so was the cut.

Bram, however, had nothing except compliments as he led her to a table in full view of a group of people sitting at another table in the corner.

When fate turned against you, it did it with a vengeance! Just about everyone from the theatre was sitting there—not just Polly and Ed McMaster, but Robin Thurgood with Cindy and Angela Tilipski and a fair sprinkling of both back and front of house staff. If she had hired a plane to sign-write in the sky, she couldn't have given her date with Bram more publicity.

'Here! Sit down!' Bram was pulling out one of the chairs from the round, glass topped bar table.

'Perhaps we should go and join the others!' In spite of her misgivings about what conclusions they had probably drawn from seeing her here with Bram, Carly nevertheless looked longingly in the direction of the group in the corner. 'They'll think we're being deliberately stand-offish!' she invented hastily.

'Don't worry!' Bram nudged the chair against her legs. 'I've already explained to them!'

'Explained!' She stopped half way to the seat. 'Explained what?'

'My dear Carly! Don't be so defensive! I merely said that we were old friends, renewing an acquaintance! What else,' he enquired blandly, 'was there to say?'

'Nothing!' Carly shook her head. 'Of course! I'm being stupid!'

Now everybody knew about the long arm of coincidence. 'My dear, what a surprise!' she could imagine Polly saying. 'You know Charlotte knew Daniel in the old days, don't you? Well, it seems she's now acquainted with our new backer. What a lucky girl she is!'

'Not stupid—tired!'

'What?' She didn't understand Bram's comment.

'I've heard Stone drives you hard!' Bram beckoned at a passing waiter.

'Only when it's justified!' Even now she was defending him. But, 'You're looking well, Bram!' She couldn't bear to go on talking about Daniel and Bram was, indeed, impressive. Everything, from the grey silk shirt to the handmade shoes to the carefully manicured finger nails spoke of money and a background of quiet wealth.

'I'm pleased you think so!' Bram said complacently. 'But now, my dear,' he drew her attention to the hovering waiter, 'what will you have to drink? A champagne cocktail?'

'Please!' Why not? Why not give the attentive group in the corner something else to talk about. Brampton Calthrop and Charlotte Mason celebrating the renewal of their friendship over champagne cocktails.

'To you, my dear!' Bram leaned across and chinked his frosted glass against hers when the drinks arrived. 'Never more beautiful!'

'Thank you!' It was not just possible but probable that Bram had actually invited the group in the corner here tonight. The thought crossed Carly's mind. Ed and Polly were well off enough but Angela certainly had no money and, as far as she knew, Robin and Cindy never went to the King Edward. And if they did, they wouldn't be drinking the expensive drinks she could see in front of them. Robin might be the theatre's public relations manager but his title, Cindy had once confided, was far more impressive than his salary.

Why shouldn't Bram have 'papered the house', not with free tickets but with free drinks to attract the audience he wanted?

'So!' Bram was leaning back and watching her. 'Have you thought about what I said this morning?'

She could pretend all night that she didn't understand but—what was the point? She knew perfectly well he was talking about her marrying Daniel. 'I've thought about it,' she acknowledged quietly.

'And?' Bram prompted.

'I'm going to marry Daniel immediately the season's finished!'

'Even though you would be making a mistake?'

Even though the moment they were out of sight, the charade would end and she and Daniel would go their separate ways. 'That,' to avoid his eye, she bent her head and drew a line in the condensation on her glass, 'is a matter of opinion!'

'No doubt!' Bram countered. 'But my opinion—if not totally without self-interest—is at least based on one established fact!'

She could hear him smiling. 'That the marriage wouldn't work!' she said.

'Something like that!' His tone made her raise brown eyes to find him watching her with absolute confidence. 'I might be wrong—appearances, of course, can always be deceptive—but I hardly think a man like Stone would be too fond of his wife if he knew that she had been single-handedly responsible for wrecking his career!'

His career! Daniel's career? Always before, it had been her future they were discussing. For a second, Carly genuinely didn't understand, but then she knew. 'But you promised!' she said. 'You promised you wouldn't back out of the season!'

'I've no intention of backing out!' Bram was all blandness; he was even a little hurt, but there was purpose behind the surface of those pale blue eyes. 'We've spent a long time working to get you an opportunity like this, my dear! What is it you're playing? Nina, Trelawney and then a part in the new Bosworth play?' She nodded dumbly. 'Exactly!' Bram was pleased. 'Just the sort of showcase of your talents we have always had in mind. Oh, no, my dear,' he drawled, 'my accident might have robbed us of your Broadway opening but nothing is going to deprive us both of this!'

Us both! Us! Carly registered. He owned her! In his eyes, he owned her. He had bought and paid for what he wanted and she had let him. And that was only money. Bram had also invested time and in all that time—in all the years since she had met him—he had never received any dividend on his investment, just the promise of that long trip through the States and his accident had deprived him of even that.

She doubted he would be as tolerant in any of the other behind the scenes fields in which he functioned. Business, politics—Bram could make or break a good many people in both of them—and she had been blind enough to think that she was different.

Ambition! Carly cringed inside. It had both lost her Daniel and blinded her to Bram.

'I know I can't make you marry me!' It must have been the strangest proposal anyone had ever had. In other circumstances, Carly might have laughed. 'I can, however, do one thing!' There was absolutely no urge to laugh as Bram went on. 'If you marry Stone, I can make sure that he never works again!'

'But how?' She was appalled. 'You can't!'

'Can't I?' There was all the confidence in the world in Bram's calm smile. 'I assure you that if you go through with this ill-judged marriage, I most definitely can!'

'But——!' She remembered the group at the corner table and lowered her suddenly high-pitched voice. 'But *how* can you do that?'

'Money!' His certainty sent a lead weight clutching at her heart. 'It's just that simple. If you have money—enough of it—you can do anything! Well,' his blue eyes ranged over her with an ironic little smile, 'almost anything! However, should you be rash enough to marry Stone, I shall see to it that every play he's approached to direct, collapses through lack of funds. On both sides of the Atlantic,' he added flatly. 'He'll become an albatross, a bad luck omen; after a while, as word gets round, no one will even want to *consider* him for a production!'

And Bram could do it. In this modern age of multinational conglomerates, his behind the scenes power and influence could easily include theatres and theatre managements. Wheels within wheels; at last Carly felt she truly understood the phrase.

'I see!' Her voice was leaden.

'I thought you would!' Bram was coolly satisfied.

'Then—what do you want?' She raised her face to his.

'My dear!' He could not have been more charming. 'I want nothing more than the reason why we're here! Waiter!' He broke off to raise a hand and the man came scurrying across. 'To have a pleasant dinner—just the two of us! Now, what would you like?' He took the proffered menu. 'I've heard the salmon's very good!'

Bram's generosity—if that was indeed the reason for the inhibiting presence of Ed and Polly and all the rest—apparently did not extend to buying dinner for them all.

At least, there was no general move to follow them as Bram guided her ahead of him into the hotel dining room and, when they came out, Carly could see through the open archway that the bar, like the old-fashioned lobby, was almost empty and quite quiet.

An early call and the need for a good night's sleep before rehearsal the following morning apparently took precedence for them as well, even if it did mean missing the last act of the real life drama that was taking place.

'May I offer you a liqueur?' Bram's fingers caressed her elbow as she stood there uncertainly.

'No! No thank you!' All she wanted—had wanted for the last hour or more—was to get away. But where?

'In that case!' Bram turned his head and a man in a chauffeur's uniform and peaked cap materialised from the shadows beside the desk. Bram nodded in his direction. 'Ralph'll drive you home!'

'Home?' Carly couldn't believe her ears. 'To the Tyler house?'

'Why not?' If anything, Bram was amused.

'But——!' She fought with the lump that choked her throat. 'Daniel's there!'

'Of course!' Bram said urbanely. 'I wouldn't like to think of you being there alone!'

'And you don't mind?' She was incredulous.

'Why should I mind if you and Stone share a house!' Had he emphasised the word share? He had. She knew it as he went smoothly on. 'In this day and age it's commonplace for an unmarried man and woman to live under the same roof! I trust you, my dear, why shouldn't I?' His eyes were guileless in a smooth, bland face. 'The house is large enough after all! How many bedrooms are there? Five?' He took her silence as his reply. 'I thought so! And now, my dear, do you have a coat with you? No? In that case, Ralph'll drive you home. I've rented a limousine,' he went on conversationally. 'It's so much more convenient than relying on cabs in a small place like this!'

Eva! It must be Eva! Against the background of his voice, Carly's thoughts went rushing on. Eva Whoever-she-was, the housekeeper. Bram had bought her. How else could he know the number of bedrooms in the house and, presumably, that two of them were being used. Had Eva also told him about the frigid atmosphere and that whenever Daniel saw her, the expression on his face matched his last name.

'Goodnight, my dear!'

'Goodnight!'

Carly sank back in the corner of the back seat as the limousine pulled away. Bram had every reason to smile as he watched her go. With Polly on his side in the theatre and now Eva in the house reporting back to him, he would know what was happening every minute of the day. Perhaps Polly also had her sights set on Hollywood and, as for Eva, who wanted to be a housekeeper all their life.

Of course Bram had no objection to her and Daniel—sharing. She fell back on his word. Bram knew exactly what was taking place.

She heard the Lincoln go off along the drive as she was walking up the front steps to the house. The door was on the catch and she opened it as quietly as she could. Far from being late, it was not quite dark outside and a light burned in the library to her left.

Daniel! Her heart did a somersault then sank and she went slowly and quietly towards the stairs.

CHAPTER NINE

THAT indefinable something that added up to spell theatre grew much stronger as the days went past. It was an increasing air of urgency and excitement but it was more than that. It was paint, make-up, wig pomade—even the smell of scorched cloth coming from the ironing board in the corner of the wardrobe added to that indescribable atmosphere.

The days themselves went both slowly and much too fast. Too fast for everything that had to be crammed in to them as the night of the first public dress rehearsal of *The Seagull* came rushing up but too slow, much much too slow, for her peace of mind.

Sometimes, she worked too hard to think and sometimes she had nothing else to do but think but, all the time, whether actively or passively, Daniel was somewhere in her mind.

'It's lovely, isn't it?'

'What?' Startled out of her reverie, Carly first glanced down at the top of Cindy's head and then at her own reflection in the long wardrobe mirror. 'Oh! Yes, it is!' She had to concentrate. She had to stop thinking about the bitter irony of a situation in which her love for Daniel and Bram's distorted love for her had trapped her.

'Do you think the train needs shortening?'

Beside her, kneeling on the floor, Cindy looked up over her mouthful of spare pins and mumbled anxiously.

'Maybe a little!' Carly tried a turn and the silk caught round her ankles. 'Yes, perhaps you're right!'

'Okay! I'll fix it!' Cindy industriously once more bent her head and started pinning: more silence, more time to think.

Love was something to which everyone aspired and yet, for her, it had become a form of refined torture. Living with Daniel, spending every leisure moment under his roof, even continuing with the charade of their impending marriage for the benefit of the cast, with her arm through his and her face happy and alive. The only thing missing, she had once realised grimly, was the ring.

Standing there, backstage in the theatre wardrobe with Cindy pinning, Carly found herself rubbing the third finger of her left hand with her thumb. It was quite bare. The ring and the wedding ring she had worn for two years had been flung angrily across a room a very long way from here and she had never seen either of them again since. It had been a diamond, large and square cut and she had got it soon after they were married.

'But it's the wrong way round!' She had raised her hand and turned it until the stone had caught the light and sent its colours flashing out in a rainbow spray.

'No, it isn't!' Daniel's lips had nibbled at her

ear and then went on and down until she forgot about the ring. 'It's quite the right way round!' How much later had it been before Daniel had resumed that particular conversation. 'It's on top of your wedding ring! This one,' he had touched the plain gold band on the hand beside his on the quilt, 'proves you're mine and this one,' he meant the diamond winking in her new engagement ring, 'proves that I'm satisfied!'

Beside her, kneeling on the floor, Cindy protested as she shifted her weight. 'Carly!'

'I'm sorry!' She made an effort to stand still. 'But how much longer do you think you're going to be?'

'Not long! About five minutes!'

Cindy didn't know, how could she, how hard it was to stand with nothing but her own reflection in the mirror for company.

The dress to which Cindy was putting the final touches was the one she was to wear in the last act of *The Seagull*. Nina had come back from Moscow pretending that she was satisfied with her life. Trigorin, the man for whom she had given up everything, had left her and she had gone on the stage but, far from stardom, life in the theatre had become a series of provincial tours but pride—whatever—Carly shrugged and Cindy once more looked crossly up, was making her pretend that that was all she wanted. The play ended with the suicide of the young man who had really loved her but the playwright, Chekhov, had called his play a comedy.

And what a comedy it was! This time Carly

managed not to shrug. Living with Daniel, although Daniel didn't want her, and spied on by Bram because he thought Daniel did.

'There! That should be better!' Cindy stabbed left-over pins into the pin cushion on her wrist and sat back on her heels. 'Try it!'

'All right!' Carly put back a leg and caught the pale silk train and turned. 'Yes,' she said, 'it is!'

In the mirror, Cindy beamed. The whole dress was hers from drawing board to pale pink silk reality. Her one entire creation of the whole play and the one which would be seen for the curtain calls. She had reason to be pleased. Carly looked down above the finely pleated bodice and the flowing lines of the skirt. With her dark hair up, she would be stunning and yet Cindy's face was totally free of jealousy.

But why should Cindy bother to be jealous? She had Robin. That morning there had been another announcement to the assembled company but this time with Robin's arm possessively around Cindy's shoulders as everyone had hung on Daniel's words.

Daniel! Her heart contracted and she looked up.

'Daniel . . .!' Her voice had a choking sound. Again and again and again, in the mirrors behind him and behind her, the image of Daniel Stone and Charlotte Mason was reflected on into infinity. 'What are you doing here?' Someone must have come up with an explanation for all that infinity. Lewis Carroll in *Alice Through the Looking Glass*, perhaps.

'What am I doing here?' Daniel was abrupt; so much for fantasy. 'I came to see the dress!'

And change it, if he wished. Cindy's expression as she knelt there was full of obvious suspense.

'But I see I have no need!' Cindy visibly relaxed. 'You look lovely, Charlotte! Just what Chekhov must have had in mind!' To anyone else it would have been a smile. To Carly, it was a sardonic twist of lips beneath steady, slate grey eyes.

'I'm glad you like it, Mr Stone!'

'What?' Daniel genuinely hadn't known Cindy had been there. But again, Carly was the only one who sensed it as Cindy scrambled, glowing, to her feet. 'Oh, yes!' Carly saw the effort as he registered. 'It's Cindy, isn't it? I think Robin's waiting for you outside!'

Perhaps Cindy at last guessed or, at least, sensed the tension in the atmosphere. At least, she took a hurried look around the room and fumbled with the pin-cushion on its elastic band around her wrist.

'Then, if you'll excuse me!' She was already half way to the door.

'Of course!' Daniel stood back, all line and muscle as he moved. 'Tell Robin that this time I'm not responsible!'

'For what?' On her way past, Cindy glanced up at him, everything about the gulf between the artistic director and a junior member of the wardrobe staff written in her puzzled face.

'For keeping you so late!' Daniel's explanation was accompanied by a smile and even Carly was affected by his charm. Cindy positively glowed. 'Tell Robin Miss Mason was responsible for that!'

'Oh! Yes, I will!' Cindy answered breathlessly. 'Goodnight, Mr Mason and Miss Stone! I mean Carly . . . I mean Mr Stone . . .!'

Confused, she disappeared on a wave of words and, once the door had shut behind her, Daniel began to move restlessly around the room. Trapped in the stays and plastic whalebone underneath the pale pink silk, Carly stood watching him.

'Carly!' When he spoke, he was musing. 'It's amazing how that name sticks, isn't it?'

'I haven't asked them to call me that, if that's what you mean!' Carly answered shortly.

'I'm sure you had no need! Here!' He saw her rigidity. 'Let me help you out of that!'

'No, no thank you! I can manage!' Carly instinctively backed away but Daniel's fingers were already at her neck, lifting the weight of hair and sending trails of memory running down her spine.

'Incidentally,' he undid the first few tiny buttons and a surgeon's fingers touched her back; cold, impassive and quite impersonal, 'did you know that Calthrop's leaving us?'

'No!' Bram hadn't told her and she was surprised. In the past few days, he had been always there; protecting his investment—with Polly's help. She often found herself wondering just exactly what it was he had promised Polly to inspire such loyalty. This time there was no mistaking what was meant as he let his eyes range pointedly over the scarcely concealing barrier of her dress. 'Well,' he said, 'at least that little comedy can now come to an end!'

'But why?' She was totally taken by surprise. 'I thought you wanted to keep it up for appearance's sake?'

'I don't think there's any need!' Daniel shrugged dismissively. 'People fall in and out of love! It happens! They live together for a while and find out that marriage wouldn't work. I think the company will be able to accept that fact of life without it totally undermining my authority!'

'I see!' She felt quite leaden. It wasn't until that moment that she realised but, while it existed, albeit just in name, their engagement had been a link—a hope—that everything was not quite dead. But now she knew.

Daniel had moved across the room and was flicking through a portfolio of costume designs for the new Bosworth play. 'We'll have to do something about finding somewhere for you to live in town!' He could have been talking about finding accommodation for a new member of the cast. 'When we do, you can move out!'

'There's no need!' She watched the pages turn. 'I can go back to Cindy and Angela's place, the room's still there!'

'No!' A page stopped in mid-turn. 'I think it would be better for everyone concerned if you lived alone—Calthrop especially!' he added as the page went on.

'And what exactly is that supposed to mean!'

She flung her head back and confronted him and he slowly lifted his. The bitterness in his eyes made her step back. 'You told me Bram was leaving,' she got out.

'You're good! You know that?' He nodded above a twisted little smile. 'You've almost got me believing that you didn't know. Okay, then, let's say for the sake of argument that Calthrop hasn't told you yet but that doesn't change the fact that he'll be back. I can hardly see him missing your first night!' He broke off to add on an aside. 'And when he does come back, I don't think he's the type to relish climbing in and out of windows or whatever he'd have to do to carry on an affair if you were living in someone else's house! And as for his hotel,' his whole face tightened, 'I won't have you going there! This theatre already has quite enough to contend with in this town without you adding that particular sort of gossip!'

'I see!' She noticed in the glass that her hands were shaking. 'So provided we're discreet, you don't mind what we do?'

'No, why should I?' Daniel closed the portfolio and stood there gazing down at it, shoulders hunched and hands thrust into his pants pockets. 'Live together—get married if you like. You're free as I recall!'

'Yes!' It had been after an argument like this that she had walked out.

It had started quietly enough. A discussion about a part Daniel had been casting in a new production, a part she knew that she could play.

She had really made an effort to be reasonable but within minutes—seconds, maybe—she had been facing him across a gulf like this and hurling accusations which she only half believed. Finally, she had been standing up, listening to the noise of her rings clattering against the wall and dropping to the floor and then she had walked out just, she saw, as Daniel was doing now.

'Goodnight, Charlotte!'

'Daniel . . .!' Why couldn't she go to him and rest her cheek against his back and put her arms around his waist. They were ten years older. Surely now she should be able to explain and have Daniel understand.

'Yes, what is it?' He kept his back towards her.

'You must believe I didn't plan all this with Bram?'

'Must I?' He turned on her savagely. 'Then I obviously can't believe the evidence of my eyes! The maidenly hesitation the night Calthrop arrived! Or,' he broke off to jibe, 'is maidenly not quite the right word to use? What was it, Charlotte? A matter of bad timing——!'

Or the sixth sense that had told her something was going to go wrong. She had never had it before or since that night but it had not only kept her from Daniel's arms, it had changed her life.

'—or was it just that you knew Calthrop was coming but he was a little too late!' He began to move towards her with long, smooth strides. 'Do you really think I didn't notice just how on edge you were!'

'Why won't you listen!' She almost screamed it

out but the words were lost as he pulled her violently into his arms and began to kiss her hard and savagely.

Some things never changed. Even now, even as his anger struck her, she felt herself begin to melt, straining up against him with her hands, still holding the bodice of her dress, crushed painfully and trapped against his chest.

And Daniel, too. She felt his anger change to passion and then to their old love as his body curved protectively around her and his hands ran down her naked spine.

'Daniel!' She breathed his name and her voice vibrated against their lips.

'What?' He raised a face heavy with wanting her and gazed down into her eyes. 'For God's sake!' He broke off to turn his head away. 'Tell him, Charlotte! Tell Calthrop when he leaves to get out of your life!'

'I——!' She stopped and felt his body stiffen and then he moved away. 'I can't!' she said.

'Which tells me everything I need to know, doesn't it?' he remarked with a vicious pleasantness. 'Goodnight, Charlotte! I know we share a house but try and keep out of my sight!'

He went and, this time, she let him go. What was the point? Would Daniel—would anyone in his mood—believe a word of what she had just been going to say? That Bram was blackmailing her!

People just didn't do such things! They might play games like pretending to fall back in love when they were just paying off old scores but people—especially someone like Brampton Calthrop III with money and power enough to attract anyone he liked—just didn't threaten insignificant actresses with the destruction of their ex-husband's career.

Carly mechanically finished taking off the pink silk dress, smoothed out the creases in the bodice and put it carefully on a hanger on the wardrobe rail. Perhaps it really would be better if she married Bram—her skin crawled—at least that would settle matters once and for all. She would be Mrs Brampton Calthrop of Boston and Palm Beach and occasionally, perhaps occasionally, of the Broadway stage and Daniel would be Daniel Stone, carrying on with a career that her marriage had bought and paid for!

The melodrama of it all even made *her* smile and, if she thought it was far-fetched, she could just imagine what Daniel's reaction would have been. He wouldn't even have given her a chance to get started! Oddly enough, though, Bram might help her. It was wild and it was crazy but it might work.

She began to think it through, dressing and leaving wardrobe automatically and pulling the door to behind her until the lock clicked home. If Bram was going to New York, it must mean that some of his other interests were crowding in on him. He played the man of leisure but, ever since she had known him, Bram had always just been going somewhere or just coming back. Even in San Francisco, he had been away in the Far East, making or breaking some government to suit his interests. He had come back, in fact, just two days before his accident.

And now he was leaving once again. She came to with a start to find herself outside the stage door with no memory of either walking through it or coming down the corridor.

What if she told Bram before he left that she would never marry him? That she was grateful— Grateful! That word again! She smiled bitterly!— but that she could never be his wife.

She began to walk across the theatre car park in the direction of the King Edward.

Bram won, he never lost—in many ways, he and Daniel were so very much alike. He had said himself he couldn't force her to marry him. Surely, *surely*, if for once, instead of fencing around the point, she came right out and told him what the situation really was, he must accept it?

And if he didn't? Her heart sank. If he didn't— she once more speeded up—she would threaten to drop out. No! She wouldn't threaten. She would mean it. If Bram said that unless she stuck to the letter of their oblique agreement, he would carry out *his* threat to ruin Daniel, she would tell him that she intended to resign from the company.

There would still be no Mrs Brampton Calthrop of Boston and Palm Beach—and occasionally, of Broadway—because she would resign and Helen, her understudy could take over. There was still a week before the first public dress rehearsal of *The Seagull* and understudy rehearsals had already been regularly taking place.

Helen could easily take over and as for Charlotte Mason—she heard the breath of her own bitter little smile—who had ever heard of Charlotte Mason anyway? Helen Anderson could equally well reap all the bouquets for succeeding as an unknown.

She had been wrong a few minutes earlier in thinking that Bram and Daniel were, in some ways, so very much alike. Daniel had always refused to sponsor her career, whereas Bram enjoyed the reflected glory. She might be an investment, just like any other, but he enjoyed seeing heads turn when she was on his arm. A wife who was a star would give him a certain glamour.

Stardom! The cause of all those bitter arguments with Daniel all those years before and now, with it almost in her grasp, here she was walking quickly and wildly thinking and absolutely ready to give it up.

'Mr Calthrop, please!' She arrived at the reception desk of the King Edward in a state that was almost breathless.

'What name shall I give?' The girl behind the desk raised cool blonde eyebrows.

'Carly—No! *Charlotte* Mason!' She drew herself up to her full height. 'Tell Mr Calthrop that Charlotte Mason would like to see him!' she caught herself before she added, 'if it's convenient!' For once she was going to face Bram on her terms. No more Carlys; no more market researched names. She had no more need to be beholden when she had nothing more to lose.

'Mr Calthrop?' Bram, at least, was there. The telephone in his suite could not have rung more than once before the receptionist was speaking. 'I'm so sorry to disturb you at this time of night!' Her voice said it was late. Her voice and a certain implication that had Carly flushing and glancing quickly at her watch. 'A Miss Mason's here to see you! A Miss Charlotte Mason! ... Yes, sir, of course. I'll have the porter show her up!'

'No, don't bother!' Carly forestalled the movement of the girl's hand towards the metal bell on the desk. 'I can find my own way!'

The receptionist and the porter, two more people knowing about her late evening visit to Bram's suite. At least the porter had no need to find out.

'It's suite five, on the top floor. The elevator's over there!' Had the girl identified her as being from the theatre? Carly didn't know but Polly did—Polly most certainly did—when she came down.

As if timed purely for Polly's benefit, the elevator doors slid open just as Polly was walking through the open archway from the bar into reception.

'Darling! What a surprise!' Polly's eyes went from Carly's face to the floor indicator above the open elevator doors. It told her nothing but then, she had no need to be told. Where else but Bram's suite could Charlotte Mason be coming from? 'I suppose Daniel's still upstairs?' Polly remarked pleasantly.

Was there a chance? Was there just a chance that those all-seeing almond eyes had been deceived and that Polly really did believe that Daniel was still with Bram? Carly held her breath. Apparently there was.

'I've always thought that having Daniel take care of the financial side of the theatre was too much to ask of him,' Polly went blandly on. 'It's bad enough to have the artistic director responsible for everything down to the washrooms in the restaurant, but money as well!' Polly gave a graceful little shrug and behind her, Carly heard the elevator doors slide shut. 'Everyone knows that money and art don't mix, don't they?'

Yes, they did. But what no one knew, no one except herself and Bram, that was, was that it had once more taken ten seconds to destroy what it had taken her ten years of her life to achieve.

'That's entirely up to you!' This time, there had been no screech of brakes as a refrigerated truck slewed violently to a halt on a San Francisco wharf. There had just been the quiet hum of air conditioning as Bram had accepted her decision to leave the company with a totally unreadable inclination of his smooth brown head. The same smooth inclination with which he had accepted her impetuous announcement that she would never—could never—marry him. 'My dear Carly,' he had got up and walked across the room to refill his glass, 'you forget one thing! I've never asked you to marry me!'

'But——!' Carly bit back on the words. There had been too many buts, too many assumptions of what had been intended. If Bram wanted to pretend, then let him. 'I'm sorry, Bram!' That phrase again and this time met with the stare of pale blue eyes.

'Don't be! But now, if you'll excuse me!' The pale blue eyes had turned towards the door.

'Of course!' Carly got hurriedly to her feet. 'But——!' Now there was a but and one she had to ask him. 'What about Daniel?' she got out awkwardly.

'What about the estimable Mr Stone?' Bram said suavely. 'I presume you're going to marry him and hope to live more or less happily ever after!'

'And you won't try and destroy him?'

'My dear Carly! What a vivid imagination! Whatever gave you that idea?' He was smiling. At least his mouth was; his eyes were like cold glass.

He had, across a table in the bar in this hotel. Carly stood and heard the cool denial and wondered if she was going mad.

'I daresay Stone will meet the usual number of problems and frustrations in the future! As you know,' they were still cold glass but now Bram's eyes were smiling, 'nothing can ever be guaranteed in the theatre!'

And never would be, not as far as Daniel was concerned. In his usual oblique way, Bram was making sure not only that she knew there indeed had been a threat but that she would never know when he might choose to put it into action.

'I see!' She paused. 'Goodbye, Bram!' And goodbye any even slight chance of staying with the company. For a few moments, she had thought it might be possible but now she knew. She had to leave and she could never marry Daniel. Those were Bram's conditions.

'Goodbye, my dear!' Satisfied, Bram had stood back and let her pass and she should, she thought, be feeling nothing except relief that the interview was over but now Polly's almond eyes were on her and on the lighted numbers in the elevator panel above her head.

'Daniel's not coming down, then?' Polly registered the fact that the elevator had stopped one floor underneath Bram's suite.

'No! There was something else they had to talk about!' She despised herself for lying as much as she despised her reason for doing it. Why should it matter if Daniel heard about this surreptitious visit to Bram's suite. She was leaving! She was leaving the company and, with it, all hope of ever going back to Daniel as his wife.

No wonder Bram had made no move to stop her. Why should he bother? She was Charlotte Mason, thirty, starting life again.

She would go back to England, she supposed, and find some job, perhaps in an office or, maybe, as a nanny; she knew nothing about anything except acting. And occasionally, in the columns of the daily papers or *The Stage* she would read some item about Brampton Calthrop or Daniel Stone.

'Then why not come and wait with us?' For a second, Polly's voice surprised her. 'Ed's there!' Polly was looking in the direction of the bar.

'We'll keep you company until Daniel *does* come down!'

Carly forced a smile. 'That's kind of you but I think I'll wait outside. I've got a headache!' What was one more lie to add to all the rest.

'You're sure?' Polly could not have been more considerate. 'Oh, well, if you insist! We'll tell Daniel where you are!' She stopped, pointedly. 'If we see him, of course, that is!'

Polly might have meant if they saw Daniel from the bar. What she actually meant was if he really was upstairs.

CHAPTER TEN

'THIRTY minutes!' Carly heard the call boy coming along the corridor, calling the half and knocking on the dressing room doors as he went past. 'Thirty minutes Miss Marshall and Miss Mason!' he called outside their door.

'Thank you!' Carly acknowledged him and, satisfied that he had been heard and they were there, she heard him go quickly on.

Thirty minutes! In fact, it was thirty-five. Thirty until the call of overture and beginners, please and then five more until the curtain actually went up.

Outside, the theatre would be beginning to fill up for this first public dress rehearsal but she wasn't nervous. It was odd. Sitting in front of her end of the long mirror, with all the naked bulbs around it switched on and blazing down and her jars and bottles of make-up set out neatly on the white cloth on the dressing table counter, Carly held out both hands and inspected them. They were absolutely steady. Perhaps she'd get more nervous when the call boy called the quarter. Surely she would. Always before she had been practically sick with stage fright before even an ordinary performance and this was a first night.

Not a first night with critics but a first night just the same with an audience out there watching as she played Nina. True, some of them were friends; if not her friends, friends of other members of the cast, and they would be sympathetic. Most of them would also be connected with the theatre and they would appreciate the ordeal of walking out on stage for the first time to present the results of weeks of work to a paying audience.

That was the purpose of public dress rehearsals. To iron out any faults and settle the cast in before the real first night.

At the last moment, for all her good intentions, she had not been able to give up Nina. Not Nina, the part she had wanted to play ever since she had been a young girl. Surely Bram would be forgiving enough to allow her that. Just Nina, just that one part and then she would leave the company.

Besides—her rationalisations had continued through many disturbed and sleepless hours—Helen wasn't ready to play Nina. Her understudy was good as Trelawney, as good as she would be herself, Carly admitted, but she was a leaden Nina. Not a seagull but a creature tied to earth.

So the letter she had written Daniel stayed undelivered. A letter of resignation with no explanation; letting him assume what he wanted about the reasons she was quitting. She had left it for him in his office when she had come in earlier that evening; perhaps that was why she felt so numb.

Who could be nervous with first night nerves

when they had just taken the step that would alter their whole life.

'There! What do you think?' Beside her at the dressing table, Madame Arkadin sat back. 'I'm not sure about the wig, though!' Polly raised two hands and ran them gracefully and lightly up over the switch which blended so perfectly and invisibly with her own reddish coloured hair under the extravagance of her flower and feather trimmed hat. 'What do you think?' she repeated edgily.

'I think it looks just right!' Her own hair had been pulled back and tied with a dull, silvery satin bow in the nape of her neck. Nina's first entrance took place in a garden and the silvery satin of her ribbon matched her dress and cloak. Her face had been left almost untouched. Just a little feathering on her dark brows, a touch of lip gloss and a dusting of powder on the few faint lines around wide-set brown eyes—the only thing, without the barrier of the footlights, which might disclose that the Charlotte Mason of flesh and blood was a good ten years older than Chekhov's heroine was meant to be.

Daniel had accepted the dark smudges underneath her eyes. 'Leave them!' he had said offhandedly. 'It makes the character more real!'

There had been some talk about their engagement making Daniel favour her to the disadvantage of other members of the cast. Carly had overheard the odd remark and seen the occasional sideways look but no one had had any need to worry. Daniel had been just as impersonal and clinical with her as he had been with everyone else during the make-up and wardrobe call earlier that afternoon.

His eyes had run over her from head to toe. 'But your skirt's too long!' he concluded dispassionately. He turned and happened to look at Cindy. 'Fix it!' he said abruptly. 'Ankle length!'

Cindy had knelt hastily at her feet and Daniel had moved on to the next in line. Emperor Stone! Even his shoulders had had an autocratic set.

That had been when Carly had decided to take her letter to his office; carefully, choosing a moment when she knew he was not there.

To deprive Daniel of theatre would be like cutting off his arm, whereas for her—she had left the letter obviously on his paper covered desk—how strange it was that something that had seemed so important for so many years now seemed so trivial.

Perhaps it was because of Nina. Playing that particular part had for so long been a goal. Now she had—or almost—and there was so much more to life. Children ... Daniel ... her heart had wrenched and, with a last look around his office, she had gone out and quietly closed the door.

Surely now, Bram would be satisfied.

'I don't know!' Polly was still fiddling with her hair. 'It feels so insecure! Have you got any bobby pins?' In the dressing table mirror, Polly looked across at her.

'No! I'm afraid not!' She had been able to pull

her own shoulder length brown hair straight
back. Just a few short wisps curled around her
forehead and at her neck; the rest was safely
tucked into a rubber band underneath the wide
silk bow.

'I think perhaps I'll go and get some, then!'
Polly stood up, all lace and satin rustling. 'God! I
wish could stop trembling!'

Carly wished that she could start or, at least,
that her whole body didn't feel like a solid lump
of lead. She tried imagining the rustling of
programmes and the expectant faces as the
audience settled in their seats but nothing altered.
She was going to ruin Nina, ruin her best chance.
Even that couldn't start the nerve ends fluttering
or her heart beating irregularly in her chest. 'You
know they've called the half?' she reminded
Polly.

'I wish I didn't!' Polly answered tragically. 'I
not only know they've called it but I know
exactly how long it is until the last act curtain
finally comes down. Three hours and seven
minutes—I'm counting them! If only I can get
through the next three hours, six minutes and
fifty-seven seconds, I'm going to be all right. I
swear, every time I *swear* that I'm never going to
put myself through this misery again, yet here I
am!' She gave a hollow laugh. 'I must say I wish
I had your coolness under fire!'

Carly smiled. For the first time, she liked
Polly. 'Appearances can . . .!' she started.

'I know! I know!' Polly finished for her, '. . . be
deceptive!' On her way to the door, she put a

hand across her mouth. 'Oh, God!' she moaned. 'I think I'm going to be sick!'

The door closed and Polly's footsteps went off along the corridor. It was quiet suddenly. While the play was actually running, the backstage loudspeaker system would be switched on so that cast members in their dressing rooms could hear when their cue was coming up but now, apart from faintly muted sounds of backstage activity, the blindingly lit room was quiet and absolutely still.

At first, the door opening, was Polly. She had found her bobby pins or she had decided she didn't need her bobby pins, but she had come back. Carly sat there and watched it opening and then she looked away. When she looked back, Daniel was standing there, reflected in the doorway behind her in the mirror, holding a sheet of paper in his hand.

'I want to know exactly what this means?' They were the first words he had addressed directly to her as a person, not as a character in a play, for several days.

'I'm resigning!' She could play games. She could pretend she had no idea what he meant and that the piece of paper could be any paper, not one with her own bald words written on it.

She wished to leave the company. Hours and hours of struggling with pen and paper had produced no more than that. For personal reasons, she was asking to resign.

Quietly and very slowly, Daniel closed the door. 'What is it? Calthrop?'

'Yes!' His face was shocking. Dark and livid beneath the mane of grey flecked hair. Carly sat and watched him come towards her.

'I see!' His breath chilled the air around her. 'I wondered why he wasn't here tonight! When are you joining him?'

She looked down at her spread fingers. 'In a few days. It depends when you release me!'

'Yes,' he said, 'I suppose it does. For once, it seems I hold the balance!'

No, Bram held that and whenever he cared to tilt it, wherever he was and whenever his devious mind decided, he could quite calmly destroy the man she loved.

'I'm not going to remind you of your contract. I see no point!' Daniel was derisive. 'He bought that, didn't he, just as he bought you when he came galloping to the rescue of this season. A million dollars, Charlotte! Are you sure you're worth it?'

He made her look up and face him in the mirror.

'But yes, I suppose you are!' he went on quietly. 'At least, I once thought so, except that I didn't think in terms of money. All I knew was that I was walking down a backstage corridor and there you were. I had to get to know you and a taxi ride just wasn't long enough! So I married you and that wasn't long enough!' His head dropped and he shook it. 'God! What a fool!'

'I did love you, Daniel!' She was treading near the edge. A bargain was a bargain, even if it had never been put into words. Bram's price included silence; he had had no need to spell that out.

'But you feel nothing now?' The words came hoarsely past her shoulder.

'No!'

'Look at me when you say that!' His palms clamped around her temples and forced her face up to confront hs. 'Look at me!' he ordered.

She shut her eyes. 'I can't!'

'Can't look at me or can't tell me you don't love me?' His husky, low-pitched question made tears prickle behind her lids.

'Please! Please let go of me!' She shook his hands away and was on her feet. 'I'm not going to marry Bram! I was not his mistress!' So much for a bargain. 'Daniel, please!'

The jaw above her tightened. 'He's got some sort of hold on you, is that it?'

'No!' She was desperate. 'I just want to leave!'

He ignored her. 'Because if it is, you don't have to tell me anything about holds!' he said intensely. 'I was caught in one for ten years. Oh, I thought I'd broken it——' Affairs, other women, he had no need to go on. '—at least, I felt so free, I even found myself thinking about re-marriage but then I saw those notices. Carly Mason! North America's new young Geraldine Page!' The rueful twist of lips above her quoted her reviews from the San Francisco papers. 'And I realised what was happening!' Daniel went on. 'You were there and I needed a replacement for this season. Fate had stepped in! Do you believe in fate, Charlotte?'

He turned her to him and she believed in everything and nothing as his body curved and lightly brushed against her.

'You are not leaving!' Each word was punctuated by his lips against her face. 'I've been a fool, we've both been foolish but I'm not ruining this chance!' His mouth moved on and up and his voice vibrated against her hair. 'I tried, God knows, I tried! I think I genuinely hated you for a while after Calthrop came back on the scene but you know what hate is?'

'Yes!' She raised her face to his and answered quietly. 'Akin to love!'

'Indeed!' His smiling eyes shone down at her. 'And when I saw that letter on my desk, I realised Calthrop's not important. What he's said, or done, or threatened, can never harm us if we stay together!'

'Not even if he's threatened to destroy you!' She had to say it.

'Destroy me? Calthrop!' Above her, his head went back on the confident brown sweep of his neck. 'Calthrop's never going to destroy me! Let him take his money—we'll find more! Let him do what he damn well likes!' He had never been more confident but, inside her stomach, the butterflies began to stir. 'I want you, Charlotte,' he went on passionately. 'I want you here— tonight—giving the performance of your life and then I want you always as Mrs Daniel Stone!'

'With children?'

'If they won't interfere with your career!'

'I told you!' She glanced down. 'You've got it in your hand.' She could just see her letter of resignation crushed between them as he held her close. 'I'm resigning from the theatre! At least,' she paused and re-thought what she had been going to say, 'I'm resigning for a while. Just long enough to . . .!'

'. . . have a family! That's right!' She watched him smile and he was Daniel, all her Daniel, as the idea took hold. 'I always told you, you'd have to be a lot older before you really came into your own as an actress. Character parts, Charlotte, your face is just too strong for anything else. I can see you in your fifties . . .!'

'Daniel!' The butterflies were getting stronger and she had to stop him.

'What?' For a moment, he looked surprised. 'I know,' he said, 'too many words!'

He stopped hers with his lips, warm and moving against her own, taking her light years away from the over-heated dressing room and suspending her in time and space.

'Damn these costumes!' His face was heavy when he raised his head. 'How can I kiss you, how can I even touch you, when I know you're going onstage!'

'Don't!' The word had been enough. Reality was there inside her and she twisted from his arms.

The butterflies had turned to raging stage-fright. She was going to be all right. She was, in Daniel's words, going to give the performance of her life and then—she once more looked up at him. His brows were drawn together as he searched her face, looking for a reason for her sudden move away.

Emperor Stone! They still had some way to go

before they reached the sort of understanding that might have stopped them wasting ten years of their lives. But they were going to do it! This time, it was she who was determined.

'I love you, Daniel!'

Along the corridor, she could hear the call boy shouting out the quarter. In fifteen minutes, she would be standing in the wings. In slightly more than twenty, she would hear her cue and she would be onstage as Nina.

He understood. 'And I love you!' he murmured softly.

But then and always she would always be exactly what she was now. Charlotte Mason. Daniel's lips came down above hers as she raised her face. Mrs Daniel Stone.

An epic novel of exotic rituals
and the lure of the Upper Amazon

THE TAKERS RIVER OF GOLD

JERRY AND S.A. AHERN

THE TAKERS are the intrepid Josh Culhane and the seductive Mary Mulrooney. These two adventurers launch an incredible journey into the Brazilian rain forest. Far upriver, the jungle yields its deepest secret—the lost city of the Amazon warrior women!

THE TAKERS series is making publishing history. Awarded *The Romantic Times* first prize for High Adventure in 1984, the opening book in the series was hailed by *The Romantic Times* as "the next trend in romance writing and reading. Highly recommended!"

Jerry and S.A. Ahern have never been better!

Share the joys and sorrows
of real-life love with
Harlequin American Romance!™

GET THIS BOOK
FREE as your introduction to
Harlequin American Romance –
an exciting series of romance
novels written especially for
the American woman of today.

Mail to:
Harlequin Reader Service

In the U.S.
2504 West Southern Ave.
Tempe, AZ 85282

In Canada
P.O. Box 2800, Postal Station A
5170 Yonge St., Willowdale, Ont. M2N 6J3

YES! I want to be one of the first to discover
Harlequin American Romance. Send me FREE and without
obligation *Twice in a Lifetime.* If you do not hear from me after I
have examined my FREE book, please send me the 4 new
Harlequin American Romances each month as soon as they
come off the presses. I understand that I will be billed only $2.25
for each book (total $9.00). There are no shipping or handling
charges. There is no minimum number of books that I have to
purchase. In fact, I may cancel this arrangement at any time.
Twice in a Lifetime is mine to keep as a FREE gift, even if I do not
buy any additional books.   154 BPA NAZJ

Name	(please print)	
Address		Apt. no.
City	State/Prov.	Zip/Postal Code

Signature (If under 18, parent or guardian must sign.)

AMR-SUB-1R

This offer is limited to one order per household and not valid to current Harlequin
American Romance subscribers. We reserve the right to exercise discretion in
granting membership. If price changes are necessary, you will be notified.